THE SONS OF NELS SWENSON

Thank you for your support!

JEANNE MARTZ

Jeanne Martz

iUniverse

THE SONS OF NELS SWENSON

Copyright © 2021 Jeanne Martz.

All rights reserved. No part of this book may be used or reproduced by any means, graphic, electronic, or mechanical, including photocopying, recording, taping or by any information storage retrieval system without the written permission of the author except in the case of brief quotations embodied in critical articles and reviews.

This is a work of fiction. All of the characters, names, incidents, organizations, and dialogue in this novel are either the products of the author's imagination or are used fictitiously.

iUniverse books may be ordered through booksellers or by contacting:

iUniverse
1663 Liberty Drive
Bloomington, IN 47403
www.iuniverse.com
844-349-9409

Because of the dynamic nature of the Internet, any web addresses or links contained in this book may have changed since publication and may no longer be valid. The views expressed in this work are solely those of the author and do not necessarily reflect the views of the publisher, and the publisher hereby disclaims any responsibility for them.

Any people depicted in stock imagery provided by Getty Images are models, and such images are being used for illustrative purposes only. Certain stock imagery © Getty Images.

ISBN: 978-1-6632-2429-3 (sc)
ISBN: 978-1-6632-2430-9 (e)

Library of Congress Control Number: 2021911524

Print information available on the last page.

iUniverse rev. date: 06/09/2021

CHAPTER 1

Mario Fontanini groped for the handrail down the steps of the school bus, his other hand holding his broken glasses, minus one lens. It was the second pair ruined in the past month. Twelve-year-old Lupita, the migrant worker's daughter, guided him off the bus.

His uncle Hans Swenson, also twelve years old and six weeks Mario's junior, lagged behind to "take care of business," namely, Bobby Bengtson, who consistently bullied Mario.

Although Mario was older than Hans, he was small in comparison to most fifth graders. And Hans had been his protector and defender since the time he had come to live at the Swenson farm, even though they had had their differences and fought occasionally.

Mario's grandmother Kinley Swenson had been expecting her late-in-life baby at the same time as his mother, Belinda, was expecting him. As the story was told to him, Hans was a surprise pregnancy for his grandmother and her new husband, Nels, back in 1980. There were complications with his mother's pregnancy from the start, and Mario was born six weeks prematurely.

School should have already been out for the summer, but five days had been added to the end of the school year calendar to make up for snow days, days the temperature dropped so low that it was unsafe for the students to stand out in the elements and wait for the school bus. The roads in Story County, Iowa, had been impassable last winter because of ice and blizzard conditions, once in early December 1992 and two other times, in January and March 1993.

"He'll just come after me again tomorrow," Mario said, as Hans rushed off the bus and joined them on the trip up the driveway. "And we still have three days of school left before summer vacation officially starts."

The bus left them in a cloud of dry dust as it moved away with Bobby, heading to his pig farm two miles down the road.

"What did you do to him?" Lupita asked with a worried look.

"I don't know. He was on the floor in the back row of seats with blood dripping from his nose the last I saw him." Hans laughed then addressed Mario, saying, "You need to start fighting your own battles with that numbskull. I'm getting tired of knocking him around for you."

"I never asked you to," Mario said. But then he thought, *I hate depending on Hans so much, but I believe he enjoys mixing it up with Bobby even though he complains.*

Lupita waved goodbye as they came to end of the long driveway. Before she disappeared behind the tall corn on the farmland adjacent to her family's mobile home, she shouted, "I hope you don't get into trouble, Hans."

Hans yelled back, "If I get suspended, I'll just start my summer vacation early and go fishing." He slapped Mario on the back. "Cheer up. Don't look so worried. You won't be the one in trouble."

Through the screen door of the farmhouse, Mario spotted his grandmother in the kitchen. The phone cord over her shoulder was stretched as far as it would reach. The hand not holding the phone was propped threateningly on her hip, and the expression on her face was not a happy one. "Uh-oh," he said. "Grandmas mad. I'm not going in there."

"Bobby must have beaten us home," said Hans, peering inside before he opened the door and tossed his books on the kitchen table.

Mario watched as his grandmother slammed the phone back in its cradle on the wall. "Hanson Joel Swenson"—both hands were on her hips now— "that was Bobby Bengtson's mother …"

"Now, Mom, before you get too mad, take a look at Mario's

glasses. Bobby broke them again. Just yanked 'em off his face, threw 'em on the ground, and stomped on 'em," Hans said, going through each motion of Bobby's actions. "Show her the glasses, Mario."

Mario shuddered as his grandmother turned and looked at him, anger still on her face. "Is that what happened, Mario?"

Hans was going to be in trouble because of him, and he didn't want to make it worse by saying the wrong thing to his grandmother, so he just looked at her wide-eyed, and nodded.

"Why did he do that to you, Mario?" his grandmother asked.

Mario shrugged in silence.

"Because Mario's little and smart, and Bobby never picks on anyone his own size," Hans answered instead.

"I'll discuss this with Nels before I decide whether to call Mrs. Bengtson back and tell her your side of the story. Right now, you two, do your chores and then hit the books. I know you have a spelling and vocabulary test tomorrow. I'll see if I can find your old glasses with the taped nosepiece, Mario. Maybe they'll get you through the end of the school year."

As the two boys were heading outside, Hans said to Mario, "I wonder what that chickenshit told his mother."

"Hanson Joel Swenson, what did you say?"

Mario trembled as his grandma came flying out the door after Hans, who was moving at rapid speed as he shouted, "I said Bobby was full of chicken spit."

"I heard you the first time. After chores, you will write all twenty of your spelling words fifteen times in cursive. And, when you're through with that, you will memorize Psalm 23 before you go to bed. Your Sunday school teacher told me it's your assignment this week for Sunday school."

After supper that night, Mario sat on the front porch with Grandma and Grandpa, watching the deer feed and drink from the pond on Uncle Tommy's farm across the road. He had heard the story of how Grandpa made Uncle Tommy a full-fledged partner in their farm business after Tommy had gotten his life back on track. Uncle Tommy was a young college student at the time Grandma married Grandpa.

Mario handed his notebook to his grandma.

"What's this?" she said. "I only meant for Hans to write his spelling twenty times, not you."

"He's in trouble because of me. It's only right," Mario said.

Grandpa was very serious. "Grandma and I decided to talk to Bobby's mother tomorrow, but we won't mention it to his dad. We don't want him to feel obligated to buy you a pair of new glasses. Bobby probably works two times harder than you and Hans because he's their only kid, and they're not able to hire help like we do with Lupita's parents."

"Why not?"

"The price of pigs isn't very good right now. In fact, we should take a load of fodder when we go to the Bengtsons' place tomorrow," Mario's grandpa said, looking at his wife.

"And I could pack up a couple of jars of peaches and pickles. We still have plenty left from last year," she replied.

"Why are you being so nice to them?" Mario asked.

"Well, we're neighbors, and neighbors need to get along. Besides, the golden rule says we're to do unto others as we would have them do unto us." Looking at Grandma, Grandpa asked, "Where's that verse located in the Bible?"

"Matthew 7:12 NKJV," Mario answered impulsively. "My mom used to say it all the time, but I thought it meant to treat other people as they treat you, meaning Bobby should get what's coming to him."

"Well, now you know." Grandpa smiled. "That's not the Lord's way."

Grandma stood up. "I'd better check on Hans. Has he finished his spelling yet?" she asked Mario.

"I had mine almost done before supper. But it's taking Hans longer because the cows wandered off to the far pasture, and with all the new calves, it was slow getting them in. It put him behind on his other chores. He's working on his Sunday school verses now."

Mario plopped down in the wicker love seat his grandma had vacated. His golden Lab, Goldie, jumped in and curled up beside him.

Grandpa reached over and scuffed Goldie's ears. "She'll soon be seven years old. I can't believe your mama's been gone that long."

"Yeah," said Mario, swallowing the lump in his throat at the mention of his mother. He could still remember the pain at her passing when he was only five, and the void she left behind still lingered in his heart to this day. The little pup Grandpa had brought home after her burial gave Mario reason to live: it was both something to love and care for and something that needed him. Even now, Goldie followed his every move.

"I talked to your other grandpa today," said his grandpa. "How do you feel about spending part of your summer with him and your dad?"

"Where is my dad now? He hasn't sent me a letter for a long time."

"Norman says he's in the Gulf of Mexico working on a big oil rig. You can stay with Norman and Emma and see your dad when he has time off. Lots of things to do down there."

"Like what?"

"Oh, like deep-sea fishing—maybe catch a swordfish or a tuna—or snorkeling among colorful fish. And they have nice resorts. What do you say?"

"Sounds fun," Mario said, but his reply lacked enthusiasm. The adventure part intrigued him, but spending time with his father always brought disappointments, letdowns, and broken promises with regard to anything he looked forward to.

"It won't be until the first of July when he comes for you. You'll have six weeks altogether with them. Grandpa Fontanini says he misses you. He hasn't seen you since last Christmas. But you don't have to go if you don't want to."

"Who will do my chores and look after Goldie and my horse Windy?"

"Don't you worry about that."

"Will I see any sea turtles? Or dolphins?" Mario asked with a little more excitement.

"I wouldn't be surprised," said his grandpa. "You'll have the rest of June and two weeks in August here at the farm before school starts again."

"Okay then. Can I call Grandpa Fontanini and tell him?"

"Only if you're sure you want to go. Do you have his number?"

"Yep," said Mario, charging inside the house with Goldie at his heels.

Kinley thumbed through the scribbled pages of Hans's spelling assignment, which was rife with erasures and crossed-out mistakes. The last two sheets were neat and orderly, so she knew Mario had helped him. "Hans, honey." She sighed. "What am I going to do with you?"

"I'm so tired, Mama," he said, "I'm not sure I can learn Psalm 23 before bedtime."

"Tell you what: There are six verses total. How about you just learn the first one tonight? One verse each day and you should have them all memorized come Sunday morning."

"Thanks, Mama. It's not fair that I get punished for protecting Mario from getting bullied, and it's not fair that I have more chores than him."

"Hans, you're being punished for using bad words, not for coming to Mario's aid. And Mario is given lighter chores because he has so many health problems."

"I know: allergies to beestings, and a fear of cows," Hans said in his husky voice, which matched his stout build. "Dad doesn't trust him to handle the cows. Mario wouldn't use a switch on one if it wandered off or to save his own life."

Kinley wrote Psalm 23:1 on a small slate and made Hans read it out loud. Each time he repeated it, she erased several keywords until there were none left on the slate. Hans had mastered the first verse.

Mario came in flying through the door past them.

"Hey, where are you going in such a hurry?" His grandma grabbed for his arm but missed.

"I have to call Grandpa Fontanini and tell him I'm going with him to the Gulf of Mexico this summer."

She smiled. "Well, that is exciting."

"It's not fair," grumbled Hans.

The next morning, the contents of the box Kinley had packed to give to Virginia Bengtson were appealing not only to the eye but also to the palate. Jars of corn, green beans, peaches, and strawberry preserves with handmade labels and attached recipes were bound to be graciously accepted and lessen the tension of her visit. What a colorful, cheery gift it made. Nels had filled the truck bed with corn husks, corncobs, and silage as his offering for Jake Bengtson.

Nels dropped Kinley off at the front door of the Bengtsons' house, then drove on past the barn. Kinley could see Bobby's father tending the pigs. She set her box down on the porch and rapped hard on the door.

It was Bobby who answered. Kinley cringed at the sight of his right eye, which was one large and swollen purple slit, and she felt an empathetic charge run down her spine.

"Oh, you poor thing," she said as Mrs. Bengtson came up behind him, wiping her hands on her apron. Kinley hadn't seen Virginia Bengtson in a while and was surprised how tired and worn the woman looked. Virginia had to be at least ten years younger than she.

"See what your boys did?" Virginia said glumly.

"Boys? Are you sure it wasn't just Hans?"

"No. Hans held him down and let Mario punch him," Virginia said, cradling Bobby from behind and brushing back the lone shaft of blond hair hanging over his forehead.

"Is that true, Bobby?" she asked.

Bobby nodded innocently; the corners of his mouth turned sadly downward, and a tear squeezed out of his good eye.

Mario isn't capable of harming a spider. What a lying little twerp.

Kinley was pretty sure Bobby hadn't been taken for emergency treatment because the family had no money. She said, "Well, I'm so sorry, Virginia. I'd be glad to pay the bills for any medical treatment Bobby incurred since it was Hans who inflicted the black eye."

"No, that won't be necessary," Virginia said. "I thought he should stay home today until the swelling goes down some. If I call the school, though, could you have one of the kids bring his school assignments home?"

"I'd be glad to. And I know this doesn't make up for what happened, but I brought a peace offering. We had an excess of canned produce from last year I'd like to share." She handed the box of goods to her neighbor. "Nels also had extra fodder he thought Jake could use."

"Thank you, Mrs. Swenson. Would you like to come in for a cup of coffee?"

"Not today, Virginia. I believe I hear Nels coming, and we have more errands to run. Feel better, Bobby."

Nels pulled up to the house, and Kinley swung into the truck's cab. "Well, that was enlightening. What did Jake have to say?"

"He never has much to say, although he isn't sure Bobby's telling the truth. And he did say that he appreciated the load of pig grub."

"Do you believe Hans held Bobby down and let Mario beat on him?"

"No! Are you kidding?"

"Virginia plans to call the school and have Bobby's homework sent home with the kids," she said.

"Then, I think one of us needs to pick them up today, or Bobby's assignments will never make it home safely on the bus ride from school. Do you think she told the school staff why Bobby didn't make it to school today?"

"I'm not sure, Nels. Bobby had a pretty ugly shiner. If you're busy this afternoon, I can pick them up."

"I would appreciate that," he said.

Kinley parked behind the school bus that afternoon so the kids would be sure to see she had come for them in the Jeep. Lupita was the first one to get in. Kinley took the opportunity to question her about the encounter with Bobby Bengtson.

"Did you see Hans hold Bobby down and let Mario hit him?"

"No, Miss Kinley. That isn't what happened. Bobby called Mario a nerd and pulled off his glasses then stepped on them. That is how they broke."

"Did Hans see him do it?"

"No, but I told him what happened, and before we got off the bus, Hans said he needed to teach Bobby a lesson. Mario and I did not see what he did to Bobby, because we got off the bus and waited for him."

"Did Hans get in trouble today?"

"I don't think so." She handed Kinley a large sealed envelope. "This is for Bobby. The principal gave it to me."

"Thank you, Lupita."

The two boys jumped in the back of the Jeep. As she pulled away from the curb, Kinley said, "We have one stop to make on our way home. Which of you wants to deliver Bobby's homework?"

"No way," said Mario. "He'd kick me around in front of his own mother."

"The bus driver reported me to the office. He told them I punched Bobby for no reason. I'll give him a good reason if I have to deliver his cootie papers," said Hans.

"I'll do it," said Lupita. "I'm not afraid of him."

Kinley handed the folder to Hans. "I elect you, Hans. All you have to say is, 'Here's your homework. Sorry about your eye.'"

"You have to be kidding?" protested Hans. "No! I won't do it."

"Yes you will," said his mother.

"Mom," whined Hans, "please don't make me."

After she pulled in to the Bengtsons' driveway, Kinley waited until Hans reluctantly got out of the Jeep. "Do it and get it over with," she demanded.

Hans approached Bobby from behind as he carried two buckets of slop toward the pigpen. Bobby set the buckets down and faced Hans, his eyes darting back and forth from Hans to Mrs. Bengtson, who was hanging clothes on the clothesline off in the distance.

"Here's your homework. And sorry about your eye, turd face. If there's a next time, it'll be both eyes."

Bobby ran off with the envelope toward his mother.

Hans got back in the Jeep.

Kinley smiled at her son. "Now that wasn't so bad, was it?"

"Nope," Hans said, hiding a smirk behind one hand.

CHAPTER 2

For Mario, the end of June came too soon. He would be leaving in a week with Grandpa Fontanini. In the meantime, early produce demanded immediate attention; peas needed picking, and cherries, raspberries, and strawberries needed preserved. Since he was not cut out for heavy farm labor, he had been assigned to the garden and to helping the women. While his grandpa, his uncle Tommy, and Hans worked in the fields, Mario and Lupita picked and shelled peas and brought in buckets of fruit for the canner.

Mrs. Morales washed, cooked, and seasoned the cleaned produce in the steamy kitchen, fighting to keep her dark hair pulled up off her neck and back from her moist forehead in a knot atop her head. She filled the canning jars, while Mario's grandma sealed and tightened the jar lids and added the jars to the pressure cooker. Their jobs were every bit as important as the men's work in the fields.

"Look how pretty," said Mrs. Morales, wiping perspiration from her brow with her apron and admiring the jars of bright fruit and peas lined up on the counter that had just come out of the canner.

"Yes," said his grandma. "Worth all the heat and sweat. Once the jars are cooled and the lids have snapped, feel free to take some back to your trailer, Carmen. You're always welcome to what's stored downstairs or to pick it fresh from the garden."

Mario and Lupita sat at the kitchen table filling another dishpan with more shelled peas. When they had finished, Mario handed the pan to Mrs. Morales while Lupita wiped off the table and took the empty pods outside to the trash.

"This is the last batch of peas, and there's nothing left on the vines," Mario said to his grandma and Mrs. Morales.

Grandma said, "What a big help you and Lupita are. Whether you know it or not, you're a big asset to running Swenson Farms. Just one more thing before you're done: The strawberries are coming on fast. If you could bring me another tub full, I'll make some freezer jam later this afternoon."

"Aw, Grandma, I wanted to take Lupita for a ride on Windy."

"You'll have all afternoon to play. It's work time for us farmers right now."

"Lupita said she'd take care of Goldie and Windy while I'm gone. I need to show her what to feed them, how to groom them, and how to exercise them. She also said she would feed the barn cats and chickens for me."

"That's a lot of work and responsibility, Lupita," said his grandma.

"That's okay. I will need something to do when Mario's gone. Besides, I like to ride Windy," Lupita answered.

"I don't know, Lupita. What do you think, Carmen?" Mario's grandma asked Mrs. Morales.

"Lupita takes care of the horses at the ranch where we stay during the winter. She is good with horses and rides very well," said Mrs. Morales.

"I guess it's all settled then. And, Lupita, you will be paid for doing the chores. Nels and I would not expect you to work for nothing. You will be doing us a favor."

"Both Windy and Goldie like Lupita. I know she will take good care of them when I'm gone. Thank you, Grandma," Mario said, giving her a quick side hug.

The supper table that night was laden with creamed peas and potatoes, a stewed hen over biscuits, and a sample of strawberry jam on warm bread.

"The crops are looking good," Grandpa said, adding a little shoptalk to the meal. "Hans and Henry hauled several loads of rocks from the bean fields. I swear they fall out of the sky. New ones appear from nowhere every year. Once the beans get too high, you can't see the rocks. They can ruin the equipment at harvesttime if not removed. Good job today, Hans."

"What's wrong, Mario?" his grandma asked. "Aren't you hungry?"

"I can hardly swallow these peas. I don't want to see another pea for a long time."

She laughed. "Don't worry. I won't serve them again before you leave, dear."

Hans asked to be excused. "I want to ride Buck for a while. My legs are tired of walking. You coming, Mario?"

Mario looked at his grandparents, unsure if they'd approve of his leaving without finishing his supper. "Is it okay?"

"Yeah," Grandpa answered. "But be back before the sun goes down."

Lupita was in the tire swing as the two boys headed for the barn to saddle the horses. "You promised to take me for a ride, Mario."

"Come on." He grabbed her hand on the way.

"I don't want to hang out with a girl," Hans said, running on ahead.

"I promised her, and she needs to know how to handle Windy because she'll be taking care of her when I'm gone."

Hans was saddled and ready to leave. "Come on, guys. I'm going to the Comstock farm. I heard one of their cows birthed four babies last night but one didn't make it. They're identical with all the same markings."

"Oh, I want to see them too." Lupita clapped with glee.

"Think you can keep up? It's a long ride from here," called Hans as he left.

"Yes, we can," Lupita yelled with determination in her voice.

Mario, immediately stopping his grooming lesson for Lupita,

threw the saddle on Windy and cinched it in place. With the aid of a booster step by Windy's stall, he swung himself into the saddle and held out his hand to Lupita. With one hand on the back of the saddle, she, in her bare feet, leaped into position behind him.

"Let's go. Hurry!" she urged.

"Not to worry. We'll catch up. Windy is much faster than Buck. Hang on!"

Although Hans had left at a gallop, they caught up quickly and followed his lead. Letting Hans lead was necessary because Mario wasn't sure which farm belonged to the Comstocks.

The Bengtson farm soon came into view, and the three of them trotted by, ignoring Bobby thumbing his nose and calling them names as they passed.

The farm with the triplet calves had quite an audience of farmers and kids of all ages who had come to see the babies and pet them—all totaled, about twenty.

After dismounting, Lupita ran toward the crowd. "Oh, muy bonito," she said, stroking the calf closest to her.

"You like that one?" said the farmer. "What did you call her?"

"*Bonito* means 'pretty' in Spanish."

"Then that will be her name!" he said. "What is your name, young lady?"

"Lupita."

"Then this one over here, trying to nurse, we'll call Lupita," he said. "Bonita and Lupita. What shall we call the other one?"

Hans spoke up: "Esmeralda."

"No, Luci," said Mario, noticing that it seemed the smallest and frailest of the three as it stumbled and vied with the others to reach an udder.

"I like Luci," said Mr. Comstock. "It goes better with Lupita and Bonita. Sorry, Hans."

Hans joined Lupita in petting the three calves and then helped Luci get to her place in the food chain. "What's the matter, Mario? Are you afraid of cow babies too?"

"No, not really. It's just I have on my Sunday jeans. My other clothes are all packed." He was really identifying with little Luci, the runt, the odd one of the three, the one that had obstacles to overcome.

Hans looked at him with a critical eye. "You're such a sissy."

The sun faded quickly as they made their way home, Hans again leading the way. Bobby Bengtson was nowhere in sight as they passed his smelly farm. Hans was about to gallop off from Mario and Lupita, but he reined Buck to a stop when he heard Windy's whinny of distress. The horse's feet thrashed the air and Lupita was thrown to the ground as Mario tried to bring the horse under control.

Bobby Bengtson dropped from the tree nearest the road and ran toward his house.

It was then that Hans knew Bobby had spooked the horse. He spurred Buck into action. As Bobby stumbled up the front steps, reaching for the door, Buck jumped three stairs, landing full force on the porch, his flared nostrils breathing heavily on Bobby's backside, before he disappeared behind a door, which slammed shut behind him.

In the process of getting inside the house, Bobby had dropped his slingshot and a handful of rocks. When Hans scooped up the weapon, he noticed the splintered boards on the porch where Buck had landed.

Before heading back to Lupita and Mario, Hans dismounted Buck and cruelly destroyed Bobby's toy of choice, chopping into tiny little pieces with an ax he'd found embedded in a tree stump that the family used for chopping firewood.

Lupita was still lying on the road in tears as Hans came back. Her left arm was severely misshapen. "That arm is broken. That's what Ralphie's arm looked like when he fell out of the hayloft, except his had the bone sticking out of the skin."

"I can't get her up on Windy, and she can't walk the rest of the way home," Mario said.

"I don't think we should move her," said Hans. "We don't want to risk hurting her further. I'll go get Dad to come with the truck."

"What if Bobby comes back while you're gone?"

"Don't worry, he's probably still in the bathroom cleaning his drawers. I threw the fear of the devil into him."

"Look at the wound on Windy's rump. It's all bloody, and some of the hair is missing," said Mario. "He must have hit her with something pretty big."

"Yeah. A rock as big as a quarter from a slingshot," Hans clarified.

Hans had never ridden Buck so fast as he did on the way to fetch his dad.

When Hans arrived with the news, his father headed for the truck with an order: "Go get Mr. and Mrs. Morales."

Lupita's parents and Kinley ran quickly to the waiting truck and climbed in. Then Nels pulled the vehicle around and headed out the driveway.

Hans followed behind on Buck.

Henry Morales lifted Lupita into the truck and stretched her out in the back seat, where Carmen Morales hovered over her daughter on their way to the nearest hospital in Ames, Iowa, ten miles away.

Kinley stayed with the boys and their horses.

"Do you want to ride Buck home, Mom?" Hans asked. "I can walk."

"It's not that far," said his mother. "You boys go home. I'm having a talk with Bobby's parents. Normally I'd let your dad take care of it, but this needs to be addressed right now."

Hans could sense her anger. "I'd like to stick around. It's getting dark, Mom, and we're the ones who saw what happened. Who knows what Bobby told his mom and dad? I think they need to see the mark on Mario's horse too."

Mario hung back in the yard while Hans and his mother pounded on the Bengtsons' door.

Hans stood by his mother's side and watched as Mr. Bengtson, in a red plaid shirt with suspenders hanging to his sides, answered the door. Some juice from his chaw of tobacco had dribbled down his chin. Mrs. Bengtson and Bobby stood looking fearful in the background.

"Mr. Bengtson, it's my understanding that Bobby fired a rock that spooked Mario's horse and caused Lupita to fall off and break her arm. She is on her way to the hospital as we speak," Kinley said in a calm, firm voice.

Mr. Bengtson turned around to look at Bobby. His booming voice shook even Hans. "What have you done, Bobby?"

"I didn't do nothing," Bobby responded, crouching behind his mother's back. "Honest, Dad, nothing."

Hans was burning with anger. "That's a lie, Mr. Bengtson. I saw him jump out of the tree. He dropped his slingshot and a handful of rocks when I chased him inside the house. You can go look at the wound on Mario's horse if you don't believe me."

Hans beckoned for Mario to come closer.

Bobby was getting panicky. "No, Dad. They were calling me names as they rode by. They said I lived in a pigsty and stunk like the pigs. I didn't mean to hurt anyone; I just wanted to scare them off. Look at the broken boards on the porch. Hans did that. He chased me onto the porch with his horse."

"That's not true, Mr. Bengtson. We didn't even see Bobby or call him names, but I did follow him up here on Buck after he fell from the tree and spooked Windy. My horse broke the boards. I do own up to that."

Kinley spoke up, saying, "Nels will come and fix the porch, Mr. Bengtson."

"What about my slingshot?" Bobby said, still hiding behind his mother's back. "Hans chopped it into a hundred pieces. He should buy me a new one."

"My dad will fix the porch, but we will not buy you another weapon, Bobby," Hans said, feeling his mother was being too soft about the situation.

"That's not fair, Mama. Tell her!" Bobby wailed.

"I'll handle this, Bobby," his father said. "And I'll deal with you later. Now, get to your room before I do it in front of the Swensons."

Bobby started to cry and shake. After having scowled at Kinley and Hans, Virginia Bengtson said, "I hope you're all happy," and she slammed the door shut.

Hans could hear an exchange of harsh words behind the door. When all was quiet, Mr. Bengtson opened the door again and stepped out onto the porch.

After examining Windy's wounds, he patted the horse's neck and said, "I'm really sorry, Mrs. Swenson. I hope the girl is okay. I'd be willing to help out with the doctor bill."

"I'll let you and Nels talk about that. Good night," she said, leading Windy away. They all walked the distance back to their farm.

"You look worried, Mom. Do you think Lupita will be okay?"

"I just hope I didn't say or do the wrong thing. Boys, this is just between us: I've heard Mr. Bengtson can be very cruel in disciplining Bobby."

"He's the kind of kid who makes you want to knock the soup out of him," said Hans.

"Maybe his behavior is a cry for attention—any kind of attention, good or bad."

"So, we just put up with his meanness? Lupita is hurt because of him," Hans argued.

"I know. It doesn't make sense. It was the right thing to tell his parents what happened. I'm sure it'll be a while before we have to deal with Bobby again. But let's pray Bobby's father uses good judgment when he punishes him."

"Like I'm going to pray for Bobby Bengtson," said Mario. "I don't care what his father does to him. I won't forgive him for what he did to Lupita."

Hans chimed in, "I'm with you, Mario."

"Did you ever think he needs or wants a friend?" his mother asked.

"It won't be us," said Hans, including Mario by gesturing with his hands. "I'm more worried about Lupita. My prayers will be for her pain and suffering, not his."

CHAPTER 3

Mario was the first on the scene when his grandpa and the Moraleses returned. The moon was high in the sky when the truck drove up the driveway. Hans and grandma followed close behind Mario.

The cast on Lupita's arm was secured in a sling, which was pressed close to her body. Her father lifted her and started to carry her to their mobile home.

"Papa, can you put me in the swing on the porch? I am not tired yet. I would like to sit in the cool air for a while."

Mrs. Morales sat down in the swing first, positioning her daughter's head against her large bosom after Mr. Morales had set Lupita down.

"How badly is it broken? Will you be able to use it at all?" Mario asked, hovering close to Lupita's side.

"Are you in a lot of pain? How long do you have to wear that thing?" Hans asked.

Lupita answered in a groggy voice, "I have to go back and have the cast removed in six weeks. I'm not feeling much pain right now. I have drugs in me."

Mrs. Morales interjected, "The doctor said she will be fuzzy for a while and that the drugs will make her sleepy."

"Lupita, you can't take care of Goldie and Windy for me now. Maybe I should stay home this summer," said Mario.

"Don't worry about that," Hans said. "It's not a big deal. I can do it."

"I will be fine in a few days," said Lupita, "and I can at least help. I don't want you to stay home because of me. Go and have a good time, Mario." She reached out with her good hand and patted his back.

"I will help with the chores also, Chica," said Mrs. Morales.

Mr. Morales had disappeared from the gathering. The sound of his old truck with a hole in the muffler could be heard coming around the side of the house on the driveway.

"Hold up there, Henry," shouted Nels, running toward the driveway. "Where are you going?"

Mr. Morales put on the brakes. "I am going to find the boy who did this to Lupita."

"Wait, Henry," yelled Grandma. She moved over to where Grandpa was standing. "Henry, I have taken care of that. I had a talk with the boy's father, and I assure you, Bobby will be punished. His father was very sorry about Lupita and offered to help with her doctor bills. It would be best if you didn't confront him. I'm afraid for the boy. His father is a cruel man and has probably already hurt him for what he did to Lupita."

"Yes, Henry," Grandpa added, "it's best not to go over there. It's very late; they are probably in bed. The doctor said Lupita will be fine. And I wouldn't want you to get arrested just because you are angry right now. Please, Henry, don't go there."

"Okay, boss. You are right. I will try and calm down, but if anything else happens to my Chica, I will not hold back my anger." He shut the truck off and wandered off toward the trailer.

"He will be okay," said Mrs. Morales as Grandma and Grandpa returned to the porch. "He just needs to be alone when he has something on his mind. He will probably go sit by the pond."

Two days after the Bobby Bengtson incident, Mario rapped on the door of the mobile home, still having reservations about leaving his personal livestock in Lupita's care. She answered in her pajamas.

Some loose strands of her dark hair had escaped from her disheveled pigtails.

"Oh, Mario, are those for me?" she said, accepting the bouquet he shyly shoved toward her. "I love the red flowers of summer. Look, they match my pajamas. Red is my favorite color."

She sniffed the flowers he had taken from his grandmother's garden without asking.

"I can't stay long because my other grandfather is here. I won't be back until a week before school starts. I just came to say goodbye. I hope you are feeling better."

"I am fine today. Please don't worry about me. Hans and I will take good care of Windy and Goldie. My mother promised to help if we need her."

"Well, goodbye then. Uh ... maybe you could keep an eye on Hans too. You know, make sure he stays out of trouble."

She laughed. "I will try my best. Have a fun vacation," she said, giving him a side hug with her good arm, still clutching the flowers.

Norman Fontanini, Mario's other grandfather, came to collect him for the summer and waited patiently as he said his goodbyes. Unlike Grandpa Swenson, Grandpa Fontanini was much taller and had a full head of salt-and-pepper hair with bushy sideburns. He had lots of money but no real home roots for very long. He called Boston home when he and Emma weren't traveling or cruising around the world.

After saying farewell and hugging Grandma and Grandpa Swenson, Mario looked around before getting in the car. "Where's Hans? I can't leave until I find him."

"I saw him go into the barn about ten minutes ago," Grandpa Fontanini said. "Don't be too long though. We have a plane to catch."

"I won't."

Mario found Hans lying in a stall with fresh hay, chewing on a piece of straw. "What are you doing?"

"Just staying out of the way. Trying to get a head start on all my extra chores," he said, with emphasis on the word *extra*. He stood up, grabbed a hayfork, and began tossing mounds of hay into the horse stalls.

"It's too late for me to back out now. My grandfather is waiting. We have to get to the airport in Des Moines. I'm sorry you're going to miss me so much," Mario added with a hint of amusement.

"Am not," said Hans.

"Can I have a hug before I go?" Mario continued to taunt Hans with a smile.

"No! Stay away from me," said Hans.

"Please," Mario persisted, moving toward him with outstretched arms and smoochie lips.

Hans pitched a load of hay in Mario's direction, covering him. "Here's your hug."

Mario laughed so hard that he toppled over and retaliated with his own pile of hay thrown at Hans.

The war was on.

Both of them were still laughing hysterically when Mario's grandfather came into the barn five minutes later.

"What's going on here? Mario, look at you. There's no time to clean up or change. Get up and let's go! Now!"

As his grandfather dragged him away, Mario blew kisses in Hans's direction. Hans covered him with another mound of hay.

"Knock it off," yelled Mario's grandfather. "Enough."

Mario brushed his clothes off before getting into the car, but as he and his grandfather drove away, he began to sneeze, and sneeze, and sneeze. *I hope Grandma didn't forget to pack my inhaler.*

Their flight from Des Moines landed on time in Corpus Christi, where Mario's step-grandmother, Emma, and his father, Tony, were waiting for them with a warm welcome. Grandma Emma had gone ahead and set up residence in a posh resort nearest to the drilling site where Mario's father could visit in his free time.

The love of his father overwhelmed Mario as he was scooped

up in his father's arms and lavished with kisses. Although it didn't make sense to him after so many months of being ignored and feeling neglected, he relished the moment by returning his own love with tearful eyes and a long, tight hug. His father was strong from working on oil rigs around the world, and because he kept an uncanny physical regimen in the gym and did many outdoor activities, namely, running and biking. He was deeply tanned from these activities, and the leathery skin around his eyes and mouth was starting to show signs of wrinkles when he smiled.

So many times, Mario had wondered about the situation between his mother and father, always thinking, *what if life had played out differently? Did their separation have anything to do with me coming between them?*

"We are going to have so much fun. Show me some muscle," said his father, setting Mario's feet back on the ground. Then he proceeded to flex his own impressive biceps, which were like something you'd find on a page in *Sports Illustrated*.

Mario mirrored his father's stance and tried to punch up the muscles in his upper arms, but there was no hint or an outline of a muscle, let alone two of them.

"Hmm, looks like you need a little work. Maybe we can go to the gym later today, after you're settled."

"Okay, but I'm dying to go snorkeling. Have you seen any sea turtles or octopuses?"

"You betcha, but you'll probably want to see them during the day. I work until sundown. It's dark before I quit."

"Don't worry," said Grandpa Fontanini. "I know exactly where to find them."

It was almost eight o'clock that night before Mario's father returned from work to collect him for their outing at the gym. Mario had combed the beach area around the resort all afternoon, then had taken a nap because he was tired from his travels and knew he would be up later than his usual bedtime.

"Sorry I'm so late, but I hitched a ride back to shore on a slow boat and grabbed a bite to eat on the way here. Are you ready, Son?"

"Sure," said Mario. "How far do we have to go?"

"Just across the plaza here. Are those the best workout clothes you've got?"

"Chores are the only exercise I get on the farm," said Mario, looking down at his baggy shorts and button-down collared shirt.

"Well, we'll have to do something about that," said his father. "Let's go." He took off in a sprint toward the after-hours sports arena.

Mario puffed and panted as he tried to keep up, glad the gym was only a short distance away. He still lagged behind while his father waited at the door. Then they went in together.

"Let's lift some weights to warm up," he said to Mario. "Let's see, these are the smallest I can find for a beginner. Give them a try, Son."

Mario used both hands to lift one weight to his chest, while his father hoisted the largest weight to his shoulders and then over his head. "I don't know, Dad. I don't think I'm meant for this."

"Do as many as you can. You'll get better and better each time we come."

"How often do you come?" Mario knew the dread in his voice wouldn't be hidden from his father. His usual daily routine didn't require much physical output—and then there was the possibility of an asthma attack.

"What's the matter? If you exercise every day, you'll start to look forward to it. The rig has a room just off the showers where I can work out. Otherwise, I start to feel sluggish after a few days."

"My arms are hurting already," Mario said. "Can I quit?"

"Okay, but give me another ten minutes. Then we can move to the treadmill."

As his father finished his weight-lifting regimen, Mario wandered around the gym. The odor of sweat-drenched T-shirts, pants, and tennis shoes reminded him of the livestock odors in the barn back home, except the gym was more contained, which made the odor stronger.

The boxing ring in the corner caught Mario's eye. He moved closer to watch. Two young men danced around each other as they sparred. Their protective headgear and drooling mouthpieces were another reminder of Windy and Buck's bridles. Mario watched intensely, captivated by the boxers' movements: quick jabs at unprotected body parts, ducking out of reach of their opponent, and steps choreographed as if part of a well-practiced dance routine.

The voice of his father broke the spell. "Would you like to learn how to do that?"

"Yes," Mario said emphatically. His thoughts and answer revolved around Bobby Bengtson, specifically, catching him off guard, staring into his eyes, and delivering a jab here and there while Bobby poked the air, missing him every time, in front of a laughing audience. *Yes. This is exactly what I need.*

"I'll talk to the manager and see if we can set something up. Shall we work on the treadmill for a while?"

"Okay. I've never done that either."

His father climbed on the treadmill and stood Mario in front of him. Mario held on to the handlebars while his father walked at a slow pace. As he increased his steps, it forced Mario to run faster and faster. Mario had a death grip on the handles, but his legs faltered under the pace.

He felt his father lifting him up with one arm, holding him off to the side, and increasing his speed.

Mario laughed so hard that he could hardly catch his breath. His father was laughing too and began gradually slowing down with all the added weight hanging off his side. When he stopped, they both collapsed into a chuckling fit.

"Dad, you are so funny."

"You liked that, huh? Want more?"

"No." Mario giggled. "I'm tired. When can I try the boxing ring?"

"I'll call my friend Angelo tomorrow. He's only here during the day. And I'll let Grandpa know. Okay?"

"Good."

Mario smiled all the way back to the hotel. He was exhausted from the trip, from the change in climate, from visiting for hours on end, and from the gym. So, when Grandma Emma told him to shower and get into his pajamas, he didn't hesitate to obey.

His father tucked him in bed, kissed him, and said goodbye. As Mario drifted off, curiosity struck. *Why did he say goodbye and not good night? It's like he's not coming back.*

CHAPTER 4

For Nels, Mario's absence had left a large void at the Swenson farm. It had been a while since he had to compute the expenditures and profits of their business using spreadsheets, then putting these into files. Stepson Tommy had introduced the computer to the farm while living with Nels and Kinley and pursuing agriculture studies at Iowa State University in Ames. Nels had been against it at first, but once Tommy set it up, it really took the load off Nels in terms of bookkeeping and also made him one of the first to use a computer in the area. Tommy's skills were also in demand from other farmers once he had started his own farm.

After sitting with Mario and watching over his shoulder in the evenings, Nels believed that his grandson was more than ready to take over the job. For a twelve-year-old, Mario was very smart and had recently made some changes for added efficiency.

Nels hated to leave a stack of stuff for Mario to do once he came home, but he knew Mario could polish it off in less than a couple of hours. He was that good. Up until now, Nels hadn't realized how much he depended on his grandson to take charge of that end of the business. His son, Hans, knew his way around computers, but mostly in game-related activities or for schoolwork. *How much longer is the kid going to be gone?*

It was Kinley who missed Mario the most. Not only was she grandmother to her daughter's precious little Mario, but she had also been the mother figure in his life for the past seven years. Belinda had come to stay at the farm after the breast cancer she had incurred while carrying Mario raged out of control a second time, taking her life. Before she passed, she had designated Kinley and Nels as Mario's legal guardians, which had been fine with Mario's father, Tony.

When the boys were born, Kinley and Nels's own son, Hans, was a robust, bouncing healthy boy, whereas Mario remained in neonatal care for the first two months of his fragile life. Both Mario and Belinda fought health issues after his birth, which limited Belinda's travels to be with Tony as he worked one job after another around the world. Tony just couldn't visualize himself in a suit occupying a desk job at home in Boston. Belinda had confided in Kinley that she refused to leave her sick baby to follow after Tony. They never had divorced but were legally separated at the time of her death.

After a long list of missed birthdays, holidays, and school activities, along with many broken promises, was it any wonder that she, as Mario's guardian and grandmother, resented any contact Mario had with Tony?

Tony and Norman Fontanini had provided well for Mario after Belinda was gone, but what blessings Tony had missed with this wonderful boy by not being around for his growing-up years. She only tolerated her son-in-law's excuses and disappointments for Mario's sake, but deep down she still hadn't forgiven him.

Hurry home, sweet Mario.

Mario had been gone for only two weeks, but Hans still grumbled as he threw a pitchfork of hay in Windy's stall.

"How hard can it be to feed Windy when you feed Buck?" his father asked.

"Well, that's only half of what she needs. I have to clean up her business so it doesn't smell or get stepped in. I have to brush her, haul in some water, you name it."

"Mario would do the same for you if you were gone."

"Like that will ever happen."

"Besides, Lupita does what she can with only one arm that doesn't involve lifting or carrying. She exercises the horse and grooms her some. She's healing well and can take over soon."

"I know. I just wonder if I'll ever get to go somewhere fun away from the farm."

"Just thank your lucky stars you haven't experienced what Mario's gone through in life. I'll see you back at the house," his father said.

Yeah, I miss the little twerp, though I'll never admit it. The one thing I do like is riding the horses with Lupita in the evening. Of course, I have to saddle them and help her on, but she's okay for a girl. She's not afraid of getting wet in the river, or finding crawdads, or baiting a fishhook, and sometimes she can even beat me when we race Buck and Windy. For a girl, she's fun to be with. Another thing I'll never admit if anyone should ask.

When he thought about it, he came to a conclusion: *Take your time, Mario. We're doing fine without you.*

CHAPTER 5

Two weeks had passed. Mario hadn't seen his father since their night at the gym. In the meantime, Grandpa and Grandma Fontanini had found ways to entertain him at the beach, gathering shells, riding the shallow waves on a boogie board, and listening to a steel band play under the palm trees while they drank fruity drinks in the shade of a cabana. The ocean brought even more delights as Mario swam with dolphins and captured underwater pictures of sea turtles while he snorkeled. The day he landed a swordfish during a deep-sea fishing trip with his grandfather had left him eager to catch an even bigger one on their next trip. This was the life. It was everything he had wanted to do and see on summer break.

But as much as Mario enjoyed the sunny shores of Corpus Christi, there was a nagging void in him. He wanted to pursue learning all he could about boxing. So, each day before any other planned outings, Grandpa would take him to the sports arena.

Since the dance of footwork captivated Mario so much, his coach paired him with an amateur boxer four inches taller than him for practice.

"Come on, kid, show me your stuff. I promise not to hurt you," said the boy, cuffing Mario on the ear.

Mario went over everything in his head that he'd learned as he danced around the young man, afraid to swing at him.

"Come on, kid." The boy punched his shoulder and moved away.

Well, I have the steps down to precision, so I'll take a chance and go for the boy's midriff.

The boy stumbled back as Mario's glove connected. After reeling for a few seconds, the boy came back swinging, but Mario was out of reach.

Wow. I did it. Better watch out, Bobby Bengtson.

After a couple more rounds, Mario's coach patted him on the back and said, "Nice work, Mario."

"Second that," said the boy, climbing out of the ring between the ropes.

Mario spent thirty minutes working out on lifting weights and running on the treadmill. Little by little, inch by inch, pound added to pound, he was doing an hour each morning. If it was important to his dad, it was going to be important to him.

Late on Saturday night, Mario spotted his father as they were gathered at the resort pool. He immediately climbed out of the water and ran into his waiting arms.

"Whoa! You've soaked my clothes," Tony said, laughing.

"Sorry, Dad. I'm glad to see you."

"That one's such a bundle of energy. It's all we can do to keep up with him," said Mario's grandfather. "I hope you're here to take him off our hands for a few days."

"I have to be back on the rig Monday morning, but we'll make every minute count, right, Son?"

"You bet, Dad."

"Look how tan you are. And do I detect the beginning of some pea-size muscles?" he said, squeezing Mario's biceps.

"Dad!" said Mario with embarrassment.

"I'm just joking," his father said, grabbing a towel and drying them both off. "Have you guys eaten dinner yet?"

"Good Lord, Tony, it's a quarter till nine," said Mario's grandfather.

"I could eat a whole pizza by myself. You want to come with me, Mario?" his father asked.

"I can always eat pizza," Mario replied.

"Not me," said Grandma Emma.

"I'm tired," his grandfather said. "You two go and have some father–son time. Here's our room key in case you get back late."

At Benny's Deep-Dish Chicago Pizza Palace, Mario selected the smallest slice of pizza from a ginormous tray. He had not eaten much pizza on the farm, but this one tasted so good, he reached for another slice.

"Now don't eat too much. We're going to the sports complex after we're done."

Mario smiled, cheese dripping off his chin. "I went this morning. I go every morning, but I have fun going with you."

"That's great, Son. Not only are you looking good, but also you have quite an appetite."

"Yeah. I'm not bothered by all the allergies I have at the farm. I think this town is good for me. I haven't used my inhaler once since I've been here. Maybe I should come more often."

"Son, the reason you are at the farm is because your mother wanted you to have a stable home and knew I couldn't give that to you. I am gone so much and never stay in one spot long enough to establish roots. It's why we were separated when she died."

"I know you weren't together when she died, but did you love her?"

"Yes, both of you so very much. I still do, Mario. Your mother had her design business that kept her in Boston. Another reason she stayed in the States is because both of you needed a lot of medical treatment after your birth. She was too ill to uproot and travel the world anymore."

"I still miss her," said Mario.

"Me too, Son." Tony stroked Mario's hair as he said it. "Do you like the farm?"

"Yeah. I have my horse, Windy, and my dog, Goldie. Hans and

I have lots of fun. Lupita is taking care of my chores and pets while I'm gone. She has a broken arm. I hope she takes good care of them."

"It sounds really nice, Son. Summer will be over before you know it. How did Lupita break her arm?"

"She was riding with me on Windy when Bobby Bengtson hit Windy with a rock from a slingshot and Lupita fell off."

"Why did he do that?"

"Because he's a bully. He always picks on me."

"I'm sorry to hear that. Do others pick on you too?"

"No, just him. I can't wait to show Hans and Lupita my pictures and what I've learned at the gym. Maybe Grandpa Nels can find time to let me work out when I get home," Mario said, dismissing the subject of Bobby Bengtson.

"Well, are we ready to hit the treadmill. Or would you rather go home since you've been at the sports complex already today?"

"No, I want to go and show you what I can do."

"Okay. Let's go," said his father, laying a twenty on the table as they left.

The gym was empty except for half a dozen regulars pounding the track around the interior, pumping iron, or riding the elliptical bike. The corner that the boxing ring occupied was dark, but Mario found a pair of gloves in his size, and his father helped him lace them up.

"Can we turn a light on over here?" Mario said to his father.

When his father switched on the lights, Mario blinked in the brightness as he stood in the center of the ring.

"Okay! Show me your stuff, Son. You're the star tonight."

Mario took a stance that balanced his weight equally on both sides and began his routine, punching at an invisible target as he circled the ropes.

"Good job. How about a little competition?" his father said.

"Really, Dad? Have you ever boxed?"

"No, but how hard can it be?" After finding a pair of gloves, his father jumped into the ring with him.

Mario hit his father's shoulder and ducked away before Tony could connect with the side of his head.

"Good job, Son." Tony made comical gestures like a cartoon character, beating the air with both fists, his head stretched backward and his legs kicking.

Mario fell on the canvas in a fit of laughter. "You are the funniest person I know."

"Here, let me help you up." His father reached out and pulled Mario into a close embrace, then led him around the ring in a waltz step.

Limp with laughter, Mario stood on Tony's feet to endure the long steps his father was taking. His face felt red and his breath became shallow. He knew the signs. He was about to have a full-blown asthma attack. His breathing stopped as he fought for air.

His father helped him down on the ring floor, a pained look on his face. "Mario, please speak to me. Do you have an inhaler with you?"

Mario pointed to his backpack in the corner of the ring.

"I'm so sorry, Son. I was just having fun. So sorry." Tony found the inhaler, put the mouthpiece between Mario's teeth, and squeezed the button to activate the device immediately.

Mario relaxed but didn't speak, his eyes fixed on the bright lamp dangling above.

"Do I need to take you to the hospital?"

Mario shook his head. "No. I'll be okay in a few minutes. I probably should go home though."

"How often does this happen? There's no hay or ragweed down here in Texas."

"Sometimes when I exercise too much, or if I laugh too hard, I can't catch my breath. That's why I have to keep my inhaler with me all the time."

"I see. Let's get you back to the hotel. We'll plan something less strenuous for tomorrow."

"You're staying?" Mario asked, excitement in his voice.

"Only for the day. I just had a great idea, and I think you'll like it."

"What is it? Where will we go?"

"It's a surprise. And I need to check with your grandpa first. Now don't get so anxious that you can't sleep tonight, okay?"

"Can you give me a clue?"

"Nope!"

"Aw, Dad, just one little hint."

Mario didn't remember falling asleep. His keen ears listened for conversation between his father and grandfather regarding tomorrow's plans, but there was too much said for him to filter out as they talked, and he finally heard no more.

Grandma Emma roused him from a deep sleep at nine o'clock the next morning. She had set the little table by the television in their room with a variety of bagels, strawberry cream cheese, juice, and coffee.

Mario's father folded the pullout bed back into the sofa, yawning and stretching, his face reflecting the start of a dark beard.

Grandpa Fontanini sat at the small table ready to eat and get going. "Come on, lazy heads. We've got big plans today. Up and at 'em," he said, buttering a bagel and smothering it with cream cheese.

"Mario, would you rather have a bowl of honey oats?" Grandma Emma asked.

"No, I'll have what they're having," he said, remembering the promised day of fun. "Are we all going?"

"Just guys today," she said. "I plan to do a little shopping."

Now his imagination carried him off again. *Guys only. Hmm.* His excitement began to build once more.

Pulling on his pants, Mario's father said, "No need to shave today. Not where we're going."

"Dad, stop! You're killing me."

His father laughed, downing a glass of orange juice. "We should be there in less than two hours if we hurry."

"What shall I wear?"

"Just regular clothes, Son. And be sure to bring sunscreen and a fresh inhaler. Are you sure you're okay after last night?"

Mario gestured with a wave in the air. "Yeah. It happens all the time. I'm used to it. It's no big deal."

"What's the worst case you remember?" his father asked seriously.

"It was my first year at the farm during harvest. I ended up in the hospital. They tested me for all kinds of allergies, and I had to start taking shots and carrying the inhaler."

"Are the attacks getting any better?"

His grandfather answered Tony's question, saying, "He may outgrow some of the allergies with time, and his immunity will build up with the shots. What he experienced last night is referred to as athletic asthma. It comes with excess activity. Even laughing too much can trigger it."

"We'll be more careful today," said Mario's father. "Let's go."

"Wherever it is, it's got me all quivering inside," said Mario.

CHAPTER 6

Dying to know their destination, Mario kept silent. A cab was waiting outside the hotel. He listened as his father ordered the driver to take them to the airport.

The cab drove to the far edge of the airfield, where a small hangar was surrounded by smaller aircrafts, helicopters, and amphibious planes.

Curiosity built at the thought of riding in any one of them. What a treat it would be to fly in a plane that could land or take off on water. It would be the ultimate thrill.

Mario's father paid the driver, and the three of them headed toward the grasshopper-green helicopter, its blades already in motion. Mario ducked close to the ground, holding on to his father's shirt sleeve, thinking his small stature could be sucked up into the whirling propellers.

Mario's father and grandfather were laughing, but he couldn't hear what they were saying because of the noise. The pilot helped him up inside and got him settled into the seat beside him. Mario's heart was ready to burst with excitement. His father and grandfather slid into the seats behind them.

"Have you figured it out yet, Mario?" his father said with a smile.

"Are we going to fly over where you work?"

"Something like that. Does that sound fun?"

"Way too cool, Dad. Have you ever been there, Grandpa?"

"No. This is my first time too."

Mario watched the ground as they lifted off. "Wow! We're going straight up." The pressure of the whirling blades caused the grass to flatten even more. Mario waved to the crew below, who grew into miniature figures against a background of runways, toy planes, and tiny buildings the higher they went. A sudden sharp turn moved his focus in another direction; they were now heading south toward the ocean.

In less than fifteen minutes, there was nothing but ocean beneath them, with no land visible in any direction for the next half hour. Mario intensely watched a small speck in the sea that came into view and grew larger as they approached. It was like a small city towering above the sea on a rig. On top of the steel structure was a flat roof marked with a large red *X*. The helicopter hovered above the spot then descended to a perfect landing.

"Where's my camera? I've got to get pictures of this," Mario said, looking back at Grandpa. "I should have been shooting all this from the start."

Grandpa handed him the camera. "Maybe you can do it on the way back."

"Good idea." He snapped pictures of the pilot, the interior of the cockpit, and the platform, and took numerous other shots as they disembarked.

"Quite a treat, huh?" his father asked.

"Yeah," Mario said, clicking more pictures as the pilot waved and the copter took off. "He's leaving us here?"

"He'll come later to take you back to Corpus Christi. I'll show you around, and we can have lunch here. There's a dining area, dorm rooms, offices, and about anything else we need. Come on, let's get started."

Mario and Grandpa Fontanini followed Tony through a maze of hallways and secured fire doors until they came to a door marked "Chief Operations Officer."

"This is my office and home for months, sometimes years, at a time. Maybe this tour will help you understand why I can't have you with me," Tony said to Mario.

"Who is the lady in the picture?" Mario asked, pointing to a photo on the desk. "She's very pretty. Is she your girlfriend?"

"Her name is Malee. She is a friend of your aunt Cherise whom I met working in the Far East."

A man in work clothes rapped on the door and entered, interrupting their conversation.

"Come in, Jonas. This is my foreman," Mario's father said, taking the hard hats Jonas handed him.

"Do you want me to give them the tour of operations, Tony?"

"No. I'll do it. This is my son and my father," Tony replied to the foreman.

"Pleased to meet you," the foreman said with a slight bow toward them before he left.

Tony followed Jonas out the door, grabbing his own protective hat with his name on it, and motioned for Mario and Grandpa Fontanini to follow. *I think Dad is glad for the interruption so he didn't have to tell me more about Malee. I'm sure she is his girlfriend. I'll ask him again later.*

Mario's father stopped before a set of double fire doors and handed Mario and Grandpa the hard hats. "You must keep these on at all times. This place is interesting, but it's also dangerous. There is a risk of fire, explosions, and collapse of platforms due to the stress and pressure of drilling and hitting gushers. It's another reason my crew must leave family behind." Looking at Mario, he continued, "Your mother used to travel with me quite often when we were first married, but she was not allowed to stay on the rig."

"And then I came along," said Mario, reviving the guilt he often felt for having been the cause of his parents' estrangement.

"Your mother had breast cancer before she was pregnant. The doctor associated her symptoms as part of her pregnancy and failed to diagnose it correctly until it was too late. Please don't ever think our separation was because of you, Mario."

"Grandpa Swenson said the same thing. But I tied her down."

"Let's just say that she preferred to be with you. She was no longer a free spirit. She had her business, her illness to cope with, and our sweet baby to care for."

"So, here we are in the middle of the ocean sitting on top of everything going on below," said Grandpa Fontanini, changing the subject.

"Yep. Drilling, pumping, filling a continual lineup of ships with crude while the supply lasts," Tony remarked.

"That's a lot of responsibility, Son."

"And it's why I can't leave. Once a well runs dry, we move to another location nearby. So, I'm constantly looking for our next move. When all the areas are tapped here, we'll be off to another part of the world."

"Fascinating," said Grandpa.

Mario was intrigued with every aspect of the operation as his dad explained how the oil was extracted from the sea, shipped to refineries, and made into products. His father allowed him to come as close as he dared to observe each phase. What fantastic stories and pictures he would have to show Hans and Lupita.

Looking at his watch, Tony said, "I think we need to get to the dining hall before Cook closes. Hobo stew is the fare of the day."

"What's hobo stew?"

"Probably yesterday's leftovers with a few new things added. It'll be good. Cook has a way of making anything tasty."

As promised, the stew was delicious. Mario asked for a second helping, much to Cook's delight, which was evident when he handed him his plate. "I'd sure like to tell my grandma back home how to make this. Do you have a recipe?"

"Never make it the same way twice. Just leftover meat. Add lots of vegetables, maybe some pasta and seasonings, and taste as you go," said Cook with a smile.

"Thanks, Cook. Maybe I'll fix it as a surprise for her."

"Here, save room for this." Cook handed him a plate with a big slab of chocolate cake with icing an inch high.

"Oh wow!" Mario said, making his eyes wide and lustful.

After he groaned from the heaviness of all the food, Tony said, "If you're full, you can take a nap, work out in the weight room, or wander around the main deck. I have some business to attend to. The copter will be here to take you to shore in about an hour. Give me a hug, big boy. I'll see you in a couple of weeks. Love you."

Mario fell into his father's outstretched arms. "Yeah, me too, Dad. I sure had fun today."

"Pop, take good care of him, and thanks for all you do. You're the best."

Mario saw tears in the corners of his father's eyes when he said it. His father did not show up again before the helicopter took off for the return trip to Corpus Christi.

The next morning after the trip to the oil rig, Mario felt he had done everything exciting he had come to see and do on the southern coast of the United States: parasailing, deep-sea fishing, snorkeling—all the activities the warm waters had to offer. He missed Goldie and Windy. He missed Hans and Lupita, but most of all he missed Grandma and Grandpa Swenson. It was hard to explain as he sifted through the wonderful collection of pictures to choose only the best of them to fill the album Grandma Emma had bought for him. The big gold letters on the front of the album read, "Summer of 1993." Inside were slots for pictures, a series of beach- and ocean-related stickers, and lines to add captions for each photo.

The two-week window of time when Mario's father had promised to come stretched into three weeks before he finally showed up. Only one week remained of Mario's summer holiday.

His father said nonchalantly, "I couldn't make it last week because one of the wells ruptured an underwater pipe and our operation had to be halted until the spill was cleaned up and the pipe fixed. As a precaution, we checked most of the other system pipes also."

"That's understandable, Tony," said Mario's grandfather. "But surely you could have called or sent a message."

"You're right, Pop. I get so caught up in my work sometimes that I can't think about anything else."

Although only twelve years old, Mario began to see the pattern to his father's parental devotion. *I wonder if that's why Mom and I moved to the farm to spend her last days. I'm sure Dad loved us, but in his own convenient way.*

Only three days were left before Mario and his grandparents were scheduled to fly back to Des Moines. Mario determined in his heart to enjoy every last minute together because he probably wouldn't see or hear from his father again until Thanksgiving or Christmas.

Mario's faithfulness to his gym regimen each day had begun to pay off. In the presence of his father, his boxing coach presented him with a small trophy inscribed with his name and the year, along with an inscription reading, "For determination and excellent skills in the sport of boxing."

The proud look on his father's face was worth every ache and pain Mario had suffered in the past five and a half weeks. There were a number of his academic trophies on the fireplace mantel next to Hans's little league and 4-H awards, but this was Mario's first sport's award, so he was even more anxious than usual to get back home to show it off.

"Dad, can you buy me a pair of boxing gloves to take home? Grandpa Nels is too busy to haul me into Ames for regular workouts, but I bet he'd build me an area in the barn where I can keep practicing."

"That sounds like a reasonable request. How many days do you have left?"

"Three days. We leave on Saturday morning."

"I'll see what I can do," he said. "Do you like clams, Mario?"

"That's an odd question. I've never tried them."

"Let's go and collect your grandpa and Grandma Emma. I know the perfect spot to spend the rest of the day. Grab your swim gear and sun lotion."

"You're so full of surprises, Dad. I can't wait to see what's next."

Back at the hotel, Mario's father whispered to Emma, then took off. From the doorway he shouted, "Meet me at the marina in half an hour."

The sun was obscured by a gray cloudy sky, which sealed in the warmth of the ocean. Grandma Emma held on to her hat as Grandpa helped her climb into the boat. The floral shirt and camera hanging around Grandpa's neck made him look like the typical tourist.

Mario dragged his hand through the water as their speedboat plowed a deep trench through the sea, which skimmed the sides of the boat. He could hardly wait to jump in and bury himself in its warm bath.

After about three quarters of an hour, a row of palm trees surfaced on the horizon out of nowhere. As the boat drew closer, Mario could see the white sandy beach surrounding them.

Tony cut the motor and drifted the craft onto shore. There were no other boats or people to share their outing. He looked around and saw the remnants of a fire, some coconut shells, and a few bottles and cans littering the pristine little island.

"Slobs," said Grandma Emma, exiting the boat and gathering the rubbish into a plastic bag. "It's people like this who ruin the beauty for the next guy to enjoy."

"Oh, what a beautiful spot, Son. I take it you've been here before?" said Grandpa Fontanini.

"Just once," said Tony. "Belinda and I came here."

Mario looked at his father. "You and Mom were here?"

"Yep. A long time ago," he said, his eyes seeming a little misty as he recalled the memory.

"Wow," Mario murmured, looking around as if standing on holy ground.

"Well, let's find a nice clean spot and dig a pit. Emma, the clams and oysters are in the cooler. And, Pop, if you'll secure the boat to that palm over there, we won't have to worry about a wave launching our ride away while we frolic." Tony laughed.

Once the food was cooked and served, Mario fought his father for the last clam.

"What about the oysters? There's plenty of them left," said his father. "I want the clam."

Mario swiftly snatched the clam. "Oysters remind me of okra—slimy and gaggy. They make me want to throw up."

"Oh yeah." His father grabbed him, ran to the edge of the water, and threw him in, after having secured the chewy morsel in the shell.

"Not fair, Dad. Child abuse! Help me, Grandpa!" yelled Mario.

His father smacked his lips and rubbed his stomach. "Yum, yum. Delicious."

"But I'm still hungry," said Mario, manufacturing a sad countenance.

"Lots of oysters left," his father reminded.

Grandma Emma produced a bag of little doughnuts and a soda. "Will this do for now?" she said, shaking the bag.

Mario, continuing the charade with a sad face, said, "Well, I suppose." He dove into the sack, stuffing his cheeks until they wouldn't hold anymore.

"Just one, please," said his father.

"Nope." Mario grinned, drooling donuts as he smiled.

Several hours after they had returned to the hotel, Mario's father disappeared as unexpectedly as he had shown up.

"He doesn't like goodbyes," said Grandpa. "It's just his way. You had a good time though, didn't you?"

"Yes, Grandpa. A wonderful time." A large box marked "Mario" sat on the table next to the boy's bed in their hotel room. He wasted no time tearing it open. There was a pair of dark burgundy boxing gloves inside. "One last surprise," he said, shaking his head and resigning himself to the fact that this was his father's way of saying "I love you."

Mario mounted the last pictures he had taken: of his boxing trophy, of their day on the deserted island, and of his father's parting gift, then closed the Summer 1993 album.

CHAPTER 7

Nels had just came in from the field when Kinley rang the supper bell. Norman, Emma, and Mario drove up the driveway at the same time.

"Hey, there's my buddy," said Nels as Mario jumped from the car before it stopped completely.

As Mario clung to him without an exchange of words, he knew the boy had missed him as much as he had longed for the boy's return.

Norman exited the car, popped the trunk, and extracted more luggage than Mario had taken on the trip.

"Whoa!" said Nels. "Will I have to build on an addition to the house to hold all this?"

Kinley and Hans ran from the back porch. Lupita jumped from the tire swing to join them, Goldie running by her side.

Kinley held Mario at arm's length before embracing him. "You look different. The ocean air must have agreed with you. You've gained weight; you're really tan; and I swear you've grown three inches."

"He still looks like the same chucklehead I remember." Hans grinned, slapping Mario's back.

"I took good care of Goldie and Windy," said Lupita, struggling to get closer to her returning friend.

Nels watched as the kids started to walk toward the house,

Mario's arm was around Lupita's neck. He playfully pulled her head to his chest. His other arm rested on Hans's left shoulder.

Mario was expressing his feelings. "I really missed you all. You're going to love the pictures I took and the things I brought back."

"Hey, you strapping young goobers, grab a suitcase or two. You can't expect us old folks to carry all this," shouted Nels to the trio as they drifted away.

Norman chuckled. "The boy was really starting to get homesick."

"Did he spend much time with Tony?" Nels asked.

"Not as much as Mario would have liked, but the time they did spent together was cherished. I'm sure you'll hear all about it. Tony does love the boy, Nels."

"How could he not?" Nels replied.

The kids returned to the pile of baggage on the lawn, and with Kinley and Emma's help, it disappeared with them into the house.

Nels offered an invitation, saying, "Kinley made Mario's favorite: pot roast and potatoes. Please join us. There's plenty to go around. The beef was freshly butchered last week."

"Thank you, Nels. It'll sure beat sitting at the airport until our flight at eight thirty," Norman replied.

"Good. I'm sure Kinley has already set two more plates on the table. Plus, the women need time to do some catching up."

The last week of summer break was a busy time for the Swenson clan. Hans had worked hard since early spring raising a young steer to enter in the 4-H Black Angus division at the Iowa State Fair, and it had paid off. He was awarded first prize for his entry, which weighed in at twenty-three hundred pounds and brought a hefty market price of three thousand dollars.

"That's a good start to your college fund," said his father.

"If I go to college," said Hans.

"What do you mean, if you go? You'll go if I have to camp out at your dorm and walk you to class every day."

Hans sensed his father's irritability with this news. "I'm not very smart when it comes to books and math. Why do I have to get a degree to be a farmer? It's what I love and what I want to do."

"Then it shouldn't be hard for you to major in some form of agriculture. Your brother Tommy got his degree at Iowa State. I figured the two of you would continue to farm our land that's been in my family for generations."

"I've got lots of time to think about it," said Hans. "What about Mario?"

"Mario is interested in a lot of things. He won't have trouble finding his place in life. I don't think he'll end up farming, though."

"Yeah. He'll probably travel the world. He really admires his father. That's all he's talked about since he's been home. It's 'my dad this' and 'my dad that.' 'Did I show you the picture of us?' Blah, blah, blah. Seems his dad's never around for the important things though. You're more of a father to him than Tony Fontanini," Hans said to his dad.

"I know, Son. I'm glad Mario had a great time with Tony. It's all still fresh in his mind. He's an intelligent kid. He'll put everything in perspective someday without your opinion on the situation. Do you understand what I'm saying?"

"Yeah. Keep my mouth shut." Hans pretended to zip his lip.

"Good," said his dad. "Now, let's go find Mom and Mario. She's anxious to take you two shopping for school clothes. You both have grown a lot this summer, not only physically but also expressively. I'm very proud of both of you."

It was early September 1993. The yellow school bus, right on time to start the new school year, was full of students eager to get back with friends and share their summer escapades with teachers and classmates.

Bobby Bengtson sat up front, cowering behind the driver. Mario thought the bruising on his face and arms looked fresh, and his hair obviously had been freshly cut by his mother. Mario glanced at Hans and quietly pointed at Bobby.

"Yeah, his mom must have put a bowl on his head and spun the chair while she buzzed him."

"No, I mean the bruises on his face," Mario whispered.

"Must have met his match," Hans replied. Then he added, "I swear, I didn't lay a hand on the kid all summer."

"He sure doesn't look very happy," Lupita said. "After he broke my arm, we never saw him again. I think he is afraid of my father."

"Or his own father," Mario interjected, remembering what Grandpa and Grandma Swenson had said about Mr. Bengtson's temper. "If Bobby starts to bully me again this semester, I want you to back off, Hans. I have a surprise for Bobby."

"What? You're going to pull your boxing gloves out of your backpack and give him what for?" Hans and Lupita laughed.

"Let's just say that if he gets too mouthy, I will put him to shame and humiliate him in front of everyone," Mario whispered. "I will dance my way to revenge."

"What? Dance, like with a tutu and tights? I can't wait to see this." Hans roared with laughter.

"Me too." Lupita covered a huge grin with the palm of her hand.

Mario saw Bobby crouch closer behind the driver as the three of them giggled and looked in his direction. At the same time, he covered the patch on the knee of his jeans with a notebook on his lap.

The second week of school was a short week because of Labor Day. Mario was disappointed that he hadn't gotten to present his summer essay to the class on Friday before the last bell rang. The teacher promised he would be the first reader when school resumed the following Tuesday.

Bobby's bruises had healed to a nasty yellow color, and his mean mouth returned once they were in school again. He called to Lupita from the bus window after the kids were dropped off at their farm, "Hey, smelly belly from Mexicali, ain't it about time for you to go back across the border where you belong?"

Hans made an attempt to jump back on the bus before the

doors closed, but Lupita stopped him. "It's okay, Hans. That does not bother me. He is just a stupid boy. I will wait for Mario's 'dance of revenge.'" She laughed.

"It's coming," said Mario, "but I won't go cruising for a bruising. I will choose my battles wisely."

"You and Bobby are poets now," Hans replied with a snicker.

Their giggles were cut short and their pace slowed after Mario saw Grandpa and Grandma waiting for them a short distance up the drive.

"Uh-oh, trouble ahead," said Hans.

Mario's heart skipped a beat. "What's going on?" But he wasn't sure he wanted to hear the answer because his grandparents were wearing the same sad expression as the day he had come home from school and found out his mother was dying. He was only five at the time, but their countenance that day was indelibly etched in his mind forever.

His grandparents encircled him with loving arms. "Mario, I just talked to your grandpa Norman. There was a terrible accident on the oil rig where your father worked; a fire on board took his life as he tried to save one of his men. I'm so sorry to tell you," said Grandpa, choking through tears as he delivered the news.

"No! No!" cried Mario, trying to struggle out of Grandpa's strong arms but failing to do so as he was being held tight. "Not my dad. We were just getting to know each other. Not my daddy. Oh, please God, no!" He sobbed, still trying to resist the grip of Grandpa's arms. Finally, once he relaxed, he switched into his grandma's embrace and cried uncontrollably.

"We'll help you through this, sweetheart," she whispered.

Lupita had dropped to the ground and covered her face with her skirt after hearing the news. She said, her teary face looking up at Mario, "I'm so sorry, Mario. We will all help you through this."

Hans joined in as they all gathered into a group hug.

Mario was limp as they slowly walked him into the house and

up the stairs to his room. "I'd like to be alone for a while," he said, falling on his bed.

"Are you sure, dear boy?" his grandpa asked. "I'd be glad to sit with you."

"Grandpa, what will happen to me?"

"This is your forever home. We are your legal guardians, and nothing will change. We will take care of you as if you were our own son, just like always."

"Will there be a funeral? Do I have to go?"

"We'll let Norman and Emma handle the arrangements. They will keep us informed. I don't want you to worry about anything. Are you sure you don't want one of us to stay with you for a while?" Grandpa brushed back Mario's hair with his rough callused hands as he talked.

"Do you think Dad suffered very much? Did he burn clear up?" Mario writhed in agony at the thought; the tears returned.

"No. Your Grandpa Norman said your father died from inhaling too much smoke. He wasn't burned badly. He rescued one guy and went back for another fellow but couldn't get him off the rig in time. They both lost their lives. They were the only fatalities before the fire was brought under control. Your father will be remembered as a hero."

"Will you buy me another dog like you did when Mama died?"

Grandpa looked at Grandma with a slight smile and, shaking his head, said, "You're not a little kid anymore, Mario. You're a big boy, and you already have a dog and a horse."

"I know. I was sort of kidding, Grandpa. I just remember how much it helped me deal with losing Mama. I would like to be alone now." He turned on his side and closed his eyes. "I'll do my chores pretty soon."

"No need for that today. You rest as much as you need. We'll feed the animals," said Grandpa.

"Come downstairs when you're ready, sweetheart, or I can bring a tray up later," Grandma said as she closed the door to Mario's room.

CHAPTER 8

Kinley did not plan to attend the funeral of her ex-son-in-law. She was conflicted about what to do. She wasn't glad Tony was gone, but she felt it would be hypocritical to mourn for him and even a betrayal to her daughter Belinda's memory. On the other hand, her dear sweet Mario needed her, needed the support of family. Although it seared her conscience, she decided to have Nels take Mario back to Corpus Christi, where Norman Fontanini had arranged for Tony's burial service. Nels was more diplomatic when it came to saying and doing the right thing.

"Nels, I think it would be nice if you took both boys," she said, broaching the subject. "Hans could be there for Mario, and it would give him a short break from the farm. The Morales family and I can handle the work while you're gone."

Nels thought for a second, then said, "Yeah, the boy sometimes thinks Mario is more privileged because he's been so many places. Since Hans has never been out of the state of Iowa, a change of scenery might be good for him too."

One week to the day after the fatal accident, the cremated body of Tony Fontanini occupied an urn at the altar of Redeemer Baptist Church of the Cross in Corpus Christi, Texas.

Nels marveled at the size of the crowd that filled the church: rows of police and firemen, local officials, and men and women from the Shell Company who worked with Tony. A large number among the crowd were just locals, having come to honor the courageous man who had risked his life to save his men.

Nels, Norman, Emma, and the two boys sat in the front row, representing Tony's small family. A young woman slipped in at the last minute. It was Cherise, who was Emma's daughter, Tony's half-sister, and Nels's niece from his first wife's family.

Cherise's presence was a surprise because of the many miles she had had to travel from the mission clinic in Myanmar.

Emma reached across the others, took her daughter's hand lovingly, and said, "When I called to tell you about Tony, I had no idea you'd show up. I'm so glad you're here."

Cherise, her long blonde hair falling over Mario's shoulders, lingered in a long embrace with him until the music started and the minister walked to the pulpit. Nels gently pulled her away and led her to a seat on the end of the aisle.

Nels glanced over at Mario, as the man whose life had been saved by Tony spoke in broken English about the courageous rescue, pausing briefly between sentences to bring his tears under control. There was not a dry eye among the company men. But Mario was listening intently, wearing the expression of a proud son.

Cherise, however, sobbed unashamedly. Nels handed her his handkerchief. "Get a hold of yourself, sweetheart. Look at Mario. He's so proud of his father. Maybe if you just think of the good things, you two shared, it would help."

"It only makes me sadder." She sniffled. "We always had so much fun together, and now he's gone," she groaned in a hushed voice, her sobs continuing.

Nels felt helpless to comfort her. As young adults, she and Tony were not only siblings but also had become best friends. Since much of Tony's work took him to the Far East, it had given them the opportunity to spend a lot of time together.

Mario stood at the back of the church with Grandpa Fontanini, who was dressed in all black except for his stiff white collared shirt.

Emma, who clung to Grandpa's arm, was also dressed in black, her light gray hair the only contrast to her outfit.

Aunt Cherise wasn't shaking many hands between wiping her red-rimmed eyes as the mourners passed by, offering their condolences and respect. Cook, the foreman, and the helicopter pilot were the only ones Mario recognized from among the mass of mourners who had come from the rig, but he tried to be a gentleman as each one shared their memories and stories about his father.

After the church cleared, Mario asked Grandpa Fontanini, "Will we bury his ashes, or will they be scattered somewhere?" He had seen movies where cremated remains were strewn across places memorable to the deceased.

"I haven't decided. What would you like to do with them?" Grandpa Fontanini replied.

"I think I'd like to take some home with me," Mario said.

"I'd like a small bottle of them too." Cherise sniffled.

"Emma and I are never in one place for very long," said Grandpa Fontanini, "and I thought about either burying them or scattering them someplace he loved."

Before he could suggest a resting spot, Mario presented an idea: "The island, Grandpa. The island where we spent our last day together."

"I think that's a perfect place. Great idea. If you all are planning to stay a day or two, I'll make the arrangements."

"We will be leaving the day after tomorrow," said Grandpa Nels.

"I can stay another day," said Cherise.

Mario held the marble urn protectively as the Fontanini clan, Grandpa Nels, and Hans left the church in a stretch limo. Since he didn't have his camera with him, Mario's mind captured the stone Baptist church's steeple and bell tower, along with the purple myrtle trees surrounding it. The scene was a peaceful sight. He hoped his hero father also felt at peace.

The director at the crematorium divided the ashes for them into three smaller vials, giving one to Mario, one to Cherise, and one to

Grandpa Fontanini. "May your loved one be at rest," he said, bidding them goodbye.

Mario wanted Grandpa Nels and Hans to experience the island as his father had introduced it to him. The family assembled the next day at the marina, where Grandpa Fontanini had rented a pontoon. Their attire was casual.

Grandma Emma had brought a cooler of clams, several lobsters (no oysters), bread, cheese, and drinks.

"Where's your shorts, Nels?" Grandpa Fontanini asked.

"Don't own a pair."

"The sea and sand get pretty hot. You're going to wish you did."

"I can take off my shirt and roll up my pant legs if need be. I'm used to the heat while working the fields."

When everyone was on board, the pontoon moved slowly through the marina. Once it reached open sea, it began to move faster.

Mario watched the excitement on Hans's face as a fine mist from the wake sprayed the side where he sat. "Hey, Grandpa Norman, can we steer the boat for a while?"

"Get over here," his grandfather replied.

The boys scrambled to his side. Mario wedged his way in between his grandfather and the steering wheel. "I already know how," he said to Hans. "Here, I'll show you."

Grandpa Fontanini stepped back and let him take over.

"See. There's nothing to it," Mario said to Hans. "You just stand here and hold the wheel on course. Watch out, though, for the whales and dolphins swimming along the side," he joked.

Hans's head jerked to the side as if expecting to see all kinds of marine life following them.

"Gotcha." Mario laughed.

As the island came into view, Grandpa Fontanini took over the controls and anchored the pontoon in the shallow ocean around the island. "Now you need to remove your shoes and socks, roll up your pants, and wade in," he directed Nels.

The boys and Cherise were already on shore before Nels slogged through the gentle waves, trying to keep his balance in the soft sand. "What an awesome view," he said, "I can see why you chose this for Tony's memorial."

Mario came over to where they were standing, and recruited Nels, Cherise, and Hans to help him dig a pit.

"How big of a hole do you need to bury one little bottle?" Hans asked.

"It's not for Dad's ashes; it's for the clams and lobsters. This is where they'll bake," Mario told Hans indignantly.

"Well, excuse me for being so stupid," Hans snapped back.

"That's okay, Son," said Nels. "I was thinking the same thing."

Cherise added grapefruit-size rocks and firewood to the pit and covered it with seaweed and a water-soaked tarp. "We'll give it a couple of hours to get nice and hot, then add the seafood."

Once their dinner was baking in the sand, Nels joined the other grandparents beneath the row of palm trees that were waving like flags amid the vast ocean. The warm breeze was restful. Nels found that if he buried his bare feet deeper down in the sand, it gave him a cool therapeutic feeling. "Ah," he said.

"You forgot a hat too," Norman chided. "You'll lose your farmer tan for sure out here."

"Okay, okay." Nels smiled. "This trip is much different than I had planned. It's good to see Mario handling this so well." He waved at the boys, who were diving into the water from the pontoon.

"Plenty of time to mourn in the days ahead," said Norman. "I am tortured inside, but I want to be strong for Mario and Cherise right now."

"When do you plan to scatter the ashes?" Nels asked.

Norman hesitated before he answered in a shaky voice, "Just before we leave the island. I'm not sure I'll ever come back here."

Mario and Emma served the meal, showing Nels and Hans how to open the shells and eat the scrumptious insides.

"Um, I could get used to these. And I love the lobster," said Hans, licking his fingers.

"Delicious," Nels commented. "My compliments to the chefs."

Cherise and Hans finished off what was left in the foil pan. "Mama," said Cherise, "we usually serve oysters with clams. It's how Tony taught me to eat them." There were tears in her eyes.

"I know. Talk to that young man." Emma nodded in Mario's direction.

"That's right. No oysters in my kitchen," he said as Cherise scowled at him.

"Shame on you. Your father should have taught you better than that," she said playfully.

Nels, having noticed Norman hadn't eaten much, said to him, away from the others, "Are you sure you're all right, Norman?"

"No. I'm just tired, Nels. We need to start cleaning up. Once we place Tony's ashes, we need to head back. It's been a long week for me and Emma."

Nels watched Mario set down the cleanup basket and throw his arms around Norman's neck. "I'm sorry about Dad. Please don't be sad, Grandpa," Mario said.

It was only the second time Nels had seen Norman get emotional since they arrived. It was as if all his strength had suddenly been depleted and he couldn't hold up any longer. Nels tried to put himself in Norman's position. What if Hans, his only son, had suddenly been taken? Although Nels and Kinley did not care that much about Tony, he began to feel guilty and phony for not having offered more help and understanding to his friend Norman.

Mario took the vial of ashes from Norman's hand. "Where shall I put them, Grandpa?"

"You pick the spot. Where do think is special?"

"Maybe along the shore and in the water where we played. Are you sure you don't want to keep any of them, Grandpa Fontanini?"

"No. Your father is here in my heart forever." He patted the left side of his chest.

Nels watched Mario open the vial and let the wind scatter its contents. What little dust remained inside, he took and buried deep beneath the palm trees.

"No one will be cooking clams under here," Mario said.

"What about your bottle of ashes, Mario?" Hans asked.

"I decided to keep them for now."

CHAPTER 9

Mario was quiet on the return trip home. Stretching out in his seat on the plane, he closed his eyes to shut out any outside interference while he sorted through his feelings. His sadness was not of the magnitude of Grandpa Fontanini's, but then Grandpa Fontanini had nearly forty years of memories to recall, whereas Mario, if he didn't count the infant and early toddler years, had less than ten years of remembrances. He did regret losing future years with his father because he knew they would have grown closer.

The way things turned out, Mario's mother had made the right decision when she established him on the farm with Grandpa and Grandma Swenson. He was loved, he was safe, and he was secure.

Grandma was at the terminal to greet them as they disembarked from the plane at the Des Moines airport. "I've missed you so much," she said, gathering all three of them in her outstretched arms.

"Everything went well," said grandpa, nuzzling his wife's neck with a day's worth of whiskers. "I'm so proud of these boys. They were true gentlemen."

Hans spoke up, saying, "Aunt Emma and Cherise send you their love."

"Oh, Cherise came?"

"Yeah," said Grandpa. "She surprised everyone."

"That's wonderful. I bet Emma was delighted. Did Cherise say whether she'll be back for the holidays?"

"She added a couple of days to her leave to spend more time with

Emma before she returns to the mission. She doubts that she can leave again this year," Grandpa said.

Mario jumped out of the car at the farm and headed for the barn.

"Whoa. Hold on there," Grandpa shouted at him.

Mario halted and turned around in time to see his grandfather glance at Grandma. She nodded to signal that it was okay.

"Well, if you're that anxious to feed the animals, then go ahead," Grandpa said.

But Mario noticed his grandparents were following him. *I bet they're going to surprise me with a puppy or a baby goat.* He ran faster.

The sight greeting him just inside the main barn door stopped him in his tracks. He was speechless as his grandparents caught up.

"What do you think?" Grandma said. Both she and Grandpa had amusement written on their faces.

"Wow! Awesome!" Two stalls had been converted into a workout area, complete with a heavy punching bag, a speed bag, a treadmill, and a second pair of boxing gloves hanging from a hook on the wall.

"We thought you'd like it better than a puppy," his Grandpa said, laughing.

"It's for both of you," said Grandma, just as Hans walked in behind them.

Mario inspected the equipment, punching rhythmically on the speed bag. "It's perfect, Grandpa. Thank you. Just the right height and everything."

"I couldn't have pulled it off without your Grandma's help."

"Oh, thank you too, Grandma. It's much better than a baby goat or a puppy."

"A baby goat?" Grandma and Grandpa echoed together.

Hans added his years of wisdom, saying, "The trouble with a baby goat is that it'll grow up to be a billy or a nanny, and then eat everything in sight."

"It was just a silly dream," Mario said. "Do you want me to teach you how to box, Hans?"

"Not now. I'm going to check on Buck, maybe take him for a trot."

"You boys finish up in here, then get your baggage upstairs and unpacked," Grandpa commanded. "I'll round up the cows and get them milked."

Grandma called out as she started toward the house, "Don't be too long. Carmen and Lupita have supper started."

Within the hour, Lupita rang the supper bell, which brought Nels and Mario from the barn and Hans racing in from the far pasture. The aroma of fresh-baked bread and apple pie loaded with cinnamon wafted through the kitchen door.

"What are we having besides bread and pie?" Hans asked, tethering Buck to a post in the front yard.

"Chicken and noodles over mashed potatoes, green beans with pearl onions, and coleslaw," said Lupita.

"What a feast," said Nels. "You know those clams we had in Texas were delicious, but I have to say I didn't get enough to fill a crow's belly. A little slice of cheese, a few crusts of bread, and a sip of wine left my stomach growling all night. Nothing like home sweet home cooking."

"You're so right, Pop," said Hans. "I had a good time, but I sure missed Mama's cooking."

Grandma greeted them at the door. "I would suggest you run upstairs and quickly change into something more suited to fine dining."

"Why?" said the guys in unison.

Grandma gestured into the dining room. "Welcome home, gentlemen."

"Another surprise?" Mario said as he stared blankly at the elegantly set table with fancy folded napkins, crystal stemware, and enough knives, forks, and spoons at each place setting to service a platoon. The best indicator of the fine dining they were in for was the antique hand-cut crystal water pitcher setting next to the tall centerpiece.

Mario's grandma looked at Lupita. "Lupita did the table all by herself. She just finished a 4-H project that taught her how to set a formal dinner table and the correct manners to go with the occasion."

"Long as the food's good," said Nels.

Hans and Mario laughed.

"Oh, you guys. Git on upstairs and dress appropriately: nice shirt, tie, clean hands and faces, and combed hair" were her final instructions.

"Yes, Mother," Nels chided Grandma.

"Hombres," said Carmen Morales, rolling her eyes and smiling.

Mario was first downstairs, dressed in his best Sunday clothes. The red gladiolas and roses of the centerpiece caught his eye. "The table is beautiful, Lupita, especially the flowers, I know they're your favorite color."

"Miss Kinley said I could pick what I wanted because they will soon be gone."

"Thank you for the welcome home," Mario said.

"I was so busy with the table, I missed seeing your reaction to the surprise in the barn," said Lupita. "Tell me, were you surprised?"

"Oh yes. I can't wait to try it out."

"Was the funeral very sad for you?"

"Yes, but I kept remembering the great summer my father and I had together. I'm so thankful it's my last memory of him."

"You are very brave. I can't imagine losing either one of my parents," she said.

Hans made his way to the table and sat down. From the waist up he looked fine, but the sandals and cutoff shorts did not impress his mother.

"Seriously, Hans. Is that the best you could do?" Grandma said. "And you, my dear husband, what's with the slicked-back gangster hair? And the clip-on tie fits under the collar, not through a buttonhole, dear."

"It's okay, Miss Kinley," Lupita said, laughing. "I believe they're hungry."

Mrs. Morales stood behind Lupita with a large bowl and spoon. "Okay, Miss Manners, what is the proper way to serve the chicken and noodles?"

"You can pass it around the table like always," said Lupita. "Thank you all for letting me practice my 4-H skills on you. Use the outside utensils first and work your way toward the plate if you wish to be proper," she said, smiling at them.

"Utensils? If we wish to be proper? You're even starting to talk fancy," Hans said. He curled his little finger as he picked up a fork.

Mario loved the warmth and happiness that continued at the dinner table. *This is my home. I wouldn't want to be anywhere else.*

The following Monday, Mario walked with Hans and Lupita to the bus stop at the end of the driveway. His grandmother had given him the option of staying home a few more days or another whole week if he needed.

There was something he wanted to do privately. After helping gather eggs and feeding the barnyard animals, he asked his grandmother's permission to take Windy out for a trot.

It was going to be one of those September days when it was raw in the morning, hot during the afternoon, and cool in the evening. He loved the change of seasons and the activities that went with it. Never a dull moment in Iowa. How could one ever be bored with the constant change?

Windy seemed to enjoy the ride as much as Mario did. Leaving the fields, they continued their ride down the gravel road that wound around to the family church.

The church was locked, and no one was around to disturb Mario's mission. He tethered Windy to a fence post, then walked up the slope to the little cemetery. Finding his mother's grave, he brushed away the fallen leaves and pulled what weeds had grown since his last visit.

Taking the vial of his father's ashes from his jacket pocket, he knelt beside the gravestone, his head bowed. "Thank you, Mama, for placing me where I would be loved and where I would be safe, a place I would grow to love and call home."

He looked heavenward, eyes open, as he searched for words to continue. "I know you and Daddy loved each other at one time. I could tell by the things he told me and the way he talked about your time together. So, I didn't think you would mind if I left his ashes here beside you, where I can visit both of you. Forgive me if I'm wrong, Mama. I hope I can be all the good things that came from each of you."

The tears needed to come, and come they did, spilling into the hole Mario had dug to place the vial of ashes. He covered the bottle and his tears with the cool earth and tamped it down, then raked a few leaves over the scar with his fingers.

His heart felt lighter as he mounted Windy. "I love you, Mama and Daddy," he said, turning Windy toward home.

Mario asked his grandmother for another day off from school when he saw the pile of homework Hans had brought home for him. The essay about the summer he had spent with his father, the one he never got to present before the tragic accident happened, still hung in the balance. It needed to be updated now. His only worry was getting through the presentation in class without breaking down emotionally. This tribute to his father would be his final farewell.

CHAPTER 10

It was late September; the fields were close to harvest. By Wednesday morning, Mario felt more than ready to return to school. A cool dewy morning greeted him, Hans, and Lupita as they walked to the bus stop. In Iowa, they call it Indian summer, when beads of moisture cling to blades of grass, spiderwebs glisten across the yard in the morning sun, and red-winged blackbirds flit to and fro to the voices of meadowlarks chirping an end-of-summer chorus.

Mario, whether it was real or imagined, felt all eyes watching him as he boarded the bus. A few kids, mainly girls with sympathetic eyes, touched his arm as he passed, saying, "Sorry about your dad."

"Thanks," he repeated several times before finding a seat.

His day went well, but shortly after lunch he began to dread the essay presentation for his last class of the day.

All his other classmates had been graded on their summer essays, so he was first on the agenda for English class. His hands and voice shook as he began, but then he relaxed after the first couple of paragraphs. Smiling, he passed around photos of sea life, parasailing, and other activities, then concluded the paper by reading the scene of the clambake on the island. His voice began to falter again. His lip quivered and the pages of his speech became clouded.

The teacher, Ms. Reed, came to his rescue and read the last paragraph as Mario took his seat and buried his face in his crossed arms on his desk.

Ms. Reed read, "The greatest summer of my life will never be relived. I will never see my father again, but I will always feel his hugs and remember what fun we shared in the summer of 1993." She laid the paper on his desk after marking it with a big red A+, and instructed the class to read their next assignment quietly for the rest of the period.

The final bell of the day rang. Mario waited until he thought everyone had left the room before he got up. Ms. Reed came over, helped him gather his things, and gave him a side hug before sending him on his way. Hans was in the hall outside the classroom. The two of them collected Lupita on their way to the bus.

Once the three of them were outside, Mario spotted Bobby Bengtson waiting at the end of the sidewalk. "Little orphan Mari-o is a crybaby. Boo-hoo-hoo! Where is your daddy now, heaven or that other place? Boo-hoo-hoo."

Hans started after Bobby, but Mario grabbed him and pushed him aside. The anger he felt in that moment let him know it was time for his dance of revenge. "I'll take care of this myself, Hans."

"Come here and say that to my face, you coward. Or are you going to run? Come on, it's just little ole me. You're not afraid of me, are you?" Mario shouted to Bobby.

Students began to gather as Mario edged closer with his challenge. Echoes of "Fight! Fight!" spread through the crowd that had accumulated.

Bobby's eyes were super vigilant, looking back and forth in all directions, as a nervous smile stretched across his lips. "Nah, I'm not afraid of you. I don't want to hurt you, that's all."

"Since when, you bully?" Mario was now face-to-face with Bobby as the circle of kids grew. "Come on, Bobby. Let me teach you a few things," he said, beginning to dance in front of him with his fists in the air.

Bobby laughed with the gang behind him.

"Don't be a chicken, Bobby. Deck him and get it over with," a voice shouted from the gang.

Bobby made a fist and swiped the air, moving past Mario's chin, as Mario danced back behind him.

"Try again, hotshot," said Mario.

Bobby lunged at Mario's midsection but lost his balance when Mario deflected the blow.

Scrambling to his feet, Bobby shouted, "You stupid jumping bean." Then he yelled to a friend, "Hey, Ralphie, help me out here!"

"Nah. This is more fun to watch," came Ralphie's voice out of the crowd.

A chorus of chants started behind Mario. "Mario! Mario! Mario!" Hans and Lupita's voices were among those who were chanting.

There was fear on Bobby's face as he stood alone, then he seemed to rally with determination as if to protect his reputation. His cheeks were red, his nostrils were flared, and his teeth were gritted in a grimace. Flipping the shaft of hair out of his eyes, he began throwing one punch after another, each one close but never connecting.

Mario moved with ease, dodging, dancing, and ducking Bobby's best efforts. He hadn't thrown one punch but had shamed Bobby something fierce. He caught sight of the bus driver and several teachers running toward the fracas.

Most of those who were gathered scattered as school officials headed to the scene."

The bus driver yelled, "All you students on my bus, get on board now!"

Bobby started to run toward the bus but was caught by the principal and ushered into the building. The school counselor took Mario without any resistance. Both boys ended up in the principal's office.

Hans and Lupita started to follow Mario, but Mr. Wheaton, the principal, ordered them to get on their bus.

"We have to wait for Mario," said Hans. "Besides, we saw the whole fight from the beginning."

"Yes, we are witnesses," said Lupita.

"Go home," said Mr. Wheaton. "I will call your parents when I get to my desk. Go, and be quick about it!" He dismissed them by pointing a finger toward the bus.

Once Mr. Wheaton had the two boys in the detention room, Bobby claimed he was the victim of Mario's advances.

In his own defense, Mario said, "Bobby insulted my father by suggesting he went to hell when he died. To me those were fighting words. I just snapped and couldn't let it pass. Hans and Lupita heard him say it."

"You're both getting a three-day suspension. I can't have fighting during or after school. You don't have to like each other, but I suggest you try to get along. Bobby, if you indeed said something that mean, you need to apologize. And, Mario, try to keep your temper under control," the principal said.

"Yes, sir," Mario replied weakly.

Bobby said nothing.

"Well, you can sit here until your parents come," said Mr. Wheaton. "I'm sure they won't be pleased to have their day interrupted." He went to his outer office to make the calls.

The phone call Kinley received was a surprise. Nels had taken her Jeep to town, so she hopped in the truck. She sped past the bus on her way to the school. Her main concern was that Mario wasn't hurt.

After parking Nels's truck along the sidewalk leading to the main entrance, she ran into the building.

The principal greeted her as she burst through his office door. "Mrs. Swenson," he said as he stood up from his desk, "sorry I had to call you. I'm sure Mario was not the instigator of this skirmish; I might have suspected as much from Hans, but not Mario. On the other hand, Bobby is in my office nearly every day, and I often think he wants to be suspended because he doesn't like school. Teachers say he has a hard time focusing and staying awake. At other times, I think it's a ploy for attention."

"I'm aware of Bobby's home situation, sir, and I know he's expected to work hard on their farm," said Kinley.

"The fact is, Mrs. Swenson, it's a 'he said, he said' sort of situation, and I must be fair in my discipline."

"How many days are you suspending them?"

"Three days each."

She looked through the window into the detention room, where the boys sat ignoring each other. "I guess that's fair. We'll certainly have a talk with Mario. He's just had so much on his mind these past weeks, especially regarding his father."

"I do have a favor to ask, Mrs. Swenson. The phone number on file for Bobby has been disconnected. Would it be asking too much for you to give him a ride home since he lives close to you?"

"I'm sure we can work something out," she said.

"Thank you for understanding, Mrs. Swenson." He knocked on the window and motioned for the boys to come out. "Okay, you two ruffians. I'll see you in three days when you check in with me, and then I don't want to see either one of you in my office for the rest of the semester. Okay?"

Bobby looked at him and smiled. "You say that every time I leave here."

"I mean it this time, Bobby."

"What will happen then?"

"Don't test me." He stuffed a letter addressed to the Bengtsons in Bobby's book bag.

"How am I supposed to get home?" Bobby asked. "It'll be past supper if I have to walk, and my dad's gonna be mad if he has to do my chores."

"Those are things you think about before you get into trouble, Bobby," said Mr. Wheaton. "However, Mrs. Swenson has agreed to give you a ride."

"No way," Mario piped in.

"Mario!" His grandmother gave him a stern look, and he said

no more. "I have Grandpa's truck. One of you can ride in the back. Mario?"

Bobby giggled. "Yes, Mario It's the Christian thing to do."

"Good luck, Mrs. Swenson," said the principal in a sympathetic tone.

Mario ran ahead and climbed in the truck bed. He pulled the neck of his knit shirt up around his mouth and nose.

Bobby walked alongside Mrs. Swenson, chatting as if they were best friends. The look on Mario's face when his grandmother opened the truck door was one of betrayal. It cut deeply into her heart.

In that same moment, she wanted to slap some sense into Bobby. The strength she mustered up to endure his lies and accusations on the way home could only have come from God himself. *Hold your peace, Kinley.*

Bobby jumped out of the truck before Kinley could turn around in the white rock driveway of the Bengtson farm. Mr. Bengtson was in the ditch along the road cutting weeds with a long-handled scythe.

"The bus broke down and Mrs. Swenson gave me a ride home," Bobby said to his father, gesturing toward the truck.

His father paused for a moment, looking at Bobby. "Would that be the same bus that rolled past here half an hour ago?"

Kinley listened as the boy lied to his father.

"Uh, I guess," said Bobby. "They must have gotten it fixed."

Kinley rolled her eyes and finished turning the truck around. She hesitated for a moment and then shouted through the open truck window at Mario: "Why don't you come up here with me?"

Mario shook his head.

"Okay be stubborn," she said, and headed toward home.

After parking the truck in the barnyard, she tried to reason with Mario as he jumped from the back end. "I know you don't understand, Mario, but …"

"No, you're the one who doesn't understand," he wailed. "Just ask Hans and Lupita what Bobby said."

Hans, eating a peanut butter and jelly sandwich, ran up to Kinley. Lupita was close behind. Mario was already gone.

"Is Mario okay?" asked Lupita. "I hope he is not in trouble."

Hans began to speak excitedly between bites: "Mom, you should have seen Mario. It was the coolest thing I've ever seen. He really shamed and embarrassed Bobby, and never hit him once. Bobby's going to need to control his mouth around Mario from now on. All the kids on the bus were laughing and talking about it."

"Yes, he did the dance of revenge," Lupita cut in with the same excitement. "He said he was saving the dance for the right moment. And what Bobby said about Mario's father was very mean. Bobby deserved to get laughed at. He is a big joke now."

"Yeah," said Hans. "I was ready to clean Bobby's plow, but Mario didn't want my help. Wow. I need to have him teach me how to box."

"Enough!" Kinley shouted. "Is your father back from town yet?"

"No. Mom, you're not going to punish Mario for defending himself, are you?"

"I will discuss it with your father. Now go do your chores."

The supper table was very quiet that evening. Mario had requested to eat alone in his room, but his grandma insisted he sit at the table.

CHAPTER 11

There was plenty of daylight left after supper. Mario was anxious to get to the barn and start teaching Hans the importance of footwork in boxing.

As they stood together in the boxing stall, it was the first time Mario had ever taken notice of Hans's oversized feet. He thought they might present a problem. "What size shoe do you wear?"

"Ten and a half. Why?" Hans answered.

"Because a boxer hardly ever stands in one place. He must move quickly and change positions constantly to avoid strikes from his opponent. It all depends on how his body weight is distributed. His hips, feet, and knees, not the arms, are what's most important when he faces his opponent. Moving the feet correctly gives him balance and stability to defend and attack with power."

"My arms are really strong, but I'm not very graceful on my feet," said Hans.

"Come over here. Stand in front of the heavy bag," said Mario. "Now, spread your feet so they are slightly wider apart than your shoulders."

Hans obeyed.

"The bag is your enemy. Put your lead foot six to eight inches in front of him. Your other foot is a little behind, and the heel should never touch the floor. Now, up on the balls of your feet."

Hans began to sway a little. "This doesn't feel right. I feel tipsy. Why on the balls of the feet?"

"It makes pivoting and changing direction much easier once you get the hang of it. Now, take short steps just at the edge of your opponent's range and move in and out." He then swung the heavy bag, forcing Hans to react.

Hans moved in the wrong direction and was knocked into a pile of hay.

"No. No. You crossed your feet. Never cross your feet over," Mario shouted.

Laughter came from the shadow of the barn door. "Grandpa, how long have you been watching?"

"Yeah, Pop. If you think that was funny, you try it." Hans giggled.

Nels replied, "I saw and heard enough that I think I could. Mario's a good teacher."

"Obviously not," said Hans. "Come on, Pop. It's your turn."

Nels followed the list of instructions out loud, standing in front of the bag. "Feet apart about shoulder width, six to eight inches out of challenger's range, on the balls of my feet, left foot behind, heel not touching the floor, and move with short steps in and out."

Hans whispered to Mario, "Let me swing the bag."

Mario nodded. Hans was right. He had a lot of strength in his arms and gave the bag a fast, wide swing. The bag came at Mario's grandpa full force.

"Whoa," yelled Grandpa, jumping to the right.

Hans stood behind the bag and pushed it quickly again, making his father scramble in the opposite direction, but not soon enough.

Grandpa lay flat on the hay while the heavy bag swung back and forth over him. He laughed hilariously. The boys joined in.

Hans laughed so hard that he had tears in his eyes. "I'm sorry, Dad. I've never seen you move so fast."

The scene was a reminder to Mario of the fun he had had with his father just months before. "Do you want to try again, Grandpa?"

"No. I learned my lesson. I'm past my ability to keep up with the young generation. Help the old man up," he said, extending a hand to each boy.

"How old are you, Grandpa?" Mario inquired.

"I'll give you two clues: Herbert Hoover was president and there were only forty-eight states when I was born."

"Boy, you are old, Grandpa. Herbert Hoover was president until 1933. You have to be at least sixty."

Hans scratched his head. "How many states do we have now?"

"Seriously, Hans. We just had that in social studies. Is that the day you got caught reading the comic book tucked inside your history book?"

Once on his feet, Grandpa turned serious. "Before you two go back to what you were doing, we need to talk."

"Uh-oh," the boys responded in unison.

"Kinley filled me in on what happened at school today. First let me say, Mario, I'm very proud of you for standing up to Bobby and defending yourself in an honorable and appropriate way. And, Hans, you did the right thing in letting Mario handle it. From my understanding, Bobby was shamed and embarrassed. From this point forward, I don't want either of you letting this incident fester into something bigger. Hopefully, Bobby learned a lesson on his own without being continually reminded by either of you."

"I wouldn't count on it, Dad," said Hans.

"Here's some good advice from an old-timer who has a lot of experience. Stay away from Bobby and ignore his unkind remarks in the future. You made your point today, so if he tries to engage you in controversy again, don't bite. Another thing: Don't rally the other kids into pestering Bobby or encourage them if they do it on their own. Think of it this way: Don't either of you become the bullies?"

"So, if one side refuses to fight, the fight is over, right?" Mario reasoned.

"That's exactly right. If you want to go a step further," said his grandfather, "be kind to him."

"Now you're going too far," said Hans.

"Well, that's what the scriptures tell us to do. 'Be kind to your enemies and by doing so, you heap coals of fire on his head.' That's from Romans 12:20 NKJV. The enemy gets a little worried and wonders what you're up to."

"I like that idea," said Mario.

"Yeah, drive him crazy," Hans said, punching Mario's arm.

Grandpa shook his head and rolled his eyes. "The motive is to keep the peace. Let's not get carried away. God knows why Bobby acts the way he does; we don't. Also, in that same chapter in Romans 12:19 NKJV, it says, '"Vengeance is Mine, I will repay," says the Lord.' The Lord will right all wrongs and bring justice in the end."

"I think Bobby's father will give him some righteous judgment tonight," said Mario. "He caught Bobby in a lie when Grandma dropped him off."

"Yes, I heard about that," Nels replied. "You've got three days plus the weekend to think things over." He picked up his hat from the hay and left.

The following Monday, Kinley drove the kids to school and accompanied Mario into Mr. Wheaton's office. Bobby was sitting in the detention room alone. Even though the window was between them, she could see the discoloration around Bobby's lip and other bruises on his arms. She wondered what his clothes were covering up.

"Oh my goodness, what happened to him?" she asked Mr. Wheaton.

"Uh, Mario, you can go to your class. I've already checked you in, buddy," he said.

Kinley watched Mario hesitate, then slowly walk out, his eyes focused on Bobby as he moved into the hallway.

"Bobby says the injuries are a result of his fight with Mario, but you and I both know those weren't there when he left here last week. I'm sending him to the school nurse to check him for other marks and bruises before I send him to class. He came in here crying this morning because the kids on the bus were giving him a hard time.

Someone said he smelled like hog manure. The kid is always clean, but I've smelled it too. I believe the odor is carried on his shoes."

"I was afraid something like this would happen," said Kinley. "The only thing bruised the day of the fight was his ego. I believe his father gave him those current bruises. Nels and I have heard how Mr. Bengtson severely disciplines Bobby. We think that is why his mother is overprotective of him."

"What a shame," the principal said, shaking his head. "I may have to report this to the authorities, but I'll wait and see what the nurse has to say."

"If there's anything I can do, Mr. Wheaton, let me know."

"Thank you, Mrs. Swenson."

Kinley left his office and drove home. She couldn't get Bobby out of her thoughts. *Nels and I did the right thing by forbidding the boys to further mix it up with Bobby. We have no idea what goes on in that child's home or in his mind. Nels will not like what I saw today.*

She drove to the field where Nels and Henry Morales were harvesting the first planting of wheat. She honked the horn to get her husband's attention over the noise of the combine, then drove to the work site without disturbing the wheat that hadn't been cut.

When Nels idled the combine and jumped off, Henry stopped the tractor pulling the wagon alongside the combine, catching the grain after it had been cut and cleaned from the stalks.

"What's going on, dear?" he asked Kinley.

"I don't know how important this is, but I thought you should know. When I walked Mario into Mr. Wheaton's office this morning, I saw Bobby in the adjoining room crying and covered with bruises and scrapes. Mr. Wheaton planned to have the school nurse check Bobby over before calling the authorities."

"Oh my God," said Nels, wincing.

"I told Mr. Wheaton we'd be glad to help in any way if he needs us."

"Thanks for stopping, sweetheart. But right now, there's nothing we can do. It'll be on my mind for the rest of the day though."

As she drove off, the five-row-head combine moved on through the field.

She had given the kids instructions to ride the bus home after school, but she fought with her conscience all day about returning to school to check with the principal about Bobby. She remembered the look on Mario's face when Mr. Wheaton sent him to class. *Dear sweet Mario. He has such a big heart. I needn't worry about him harassing Bobby.*

When the bus came to a stop at the farm and dropped off the kids, Kinley was tending her garden along the driveway. She stood as they approached. "Well, how did it go today?"

"Fine," said Mario.

"Did Bobby cause any more trouble?" she asked, getting right to the point, eager to know any details.

"Nah," said Hans. "He kind of kept to himself, but after recess, he disappeared and they were looking for him."

Mario added, "I saw him sitting over behind the backstop at home plate all alone at recess. No one was using the ballfield. I kind of felt sorry for him, but I just left him alone. That's the last time anyone saw him."

"Where do you think he went?" Kinley asked.

"Who cares," Lupita piped in. "I am still having trouble with my arm because of him. I hate him."

"Someone really beat the stuffing out of him," said Mario with a worried, sympathetic look. "He had bruises all over him."

"If he ever hurts me again, my father will probably kill him," said Lupita.

"*Hate, beat, kill.* Please don't use those words in my presence in regard to another person," Kinley replied firmly to the three of them.

"Sorry, Miss Kinley. I will try."

Two weeks had passed and Bobby Bengtson had not been seen. Principal Wheaton called the Swensons late in the afternoon to ask a favor.

"Mrs. Swenson, the last time we spoke, you offered your help, if needed, with Bobby Bengtson. After I spoke with the child advocate authorities, and after their subsequent visit to the home, Bobby has not been back to school. At first, I assumed the parents had pulled him from school, but on a follow-up visit by the truant officer, no one answered the door. He wrote on his report, 'Except for the squealing pigs, the place seemed abandoned.'"

"What can we do to help?" Kinley asked.

"Could you check with some of the other neighbors and see if they can shed any light on what's happening at the Bengtsons'? I'd like to know what the parents' intentions are for Bobby."

"My husband should be here soon. I'll have him take a look around the place and check with the other farmers in the area. Mr. Bengtson and Nels get along okay. Since it's late, I'll call you, or have Nels call you, in the morning."

"Thank you, Mrs. Swenson." She hung up the phone and pondered their conversation. *Something is really wrong. I can feel it.* Then she prayed for Bobby and his family.

CHAPTER 12

Nels met Kinley coming out the door when he came home that night.

"Thank goodness you're home. Mr. Wheaton called and asked us to check on the Bengtsons. There's something bad going on there. I was about to go myself."

"Calm down, dear. I drove by the place this morning and didn't notice anything amiss. It's too dark to look around now. I promise that I'll go first thing in the morning."

"I'm not sure I can sleep not knowing, but you're right. I'll warm up some supper," she said.

Nels could hear the pigs squealing before he even entered the Bengtsons' property, and he knew pigs only reacted that way when they were in danger or hungry. Mr. Bengtson's old rusted truck was nowhere in sight. Weeds had taken over the place. The smell was atrocious.

He knocked on the door but got no response. Trying the door handle, he found it was unlocked, so he opened the door and shouted, "Anybody home?"

The inside was neat and clean as if the occupants had suddenly been snatched away or left on a holiday. He shouted again, "It's Nels Swenson. I'd like to talk to you." An eerie feeling swept over him; he backed out of the house rather than going farther inside. A rifle resting next to the door fell to the floor when he brushed against it.

He propped it up in the same spot where it had been and shut the door behind him.

Glad to be back in the open air even though it smelled foul, he headed toward the noisy pigpen. The closer he came to the pigsty, the more the stench of pig manure and other, unidentifiable odors overwhelmed him.

A few feet closer and the problem became clear. Flies were swarming over dead hog carcasses, which were mired in the muck of the pen. A herd of skinny pigs with protruding ribs and sharply defined backbones wallowed around their fallen brothers and sisters, rooting for a bite of something from their remains.

"Oh my God, it's worse than I could have ever imagined," Nels said out loud. His first instinct was to feed the starving lot of pigs. He loaded fodder from Bengtson's barn into his truck, drove back to the pigpen, and shoveled two loads into the confinement.

He watched as the pigs fed. One big boar stood out from the crowd, fatter and healthier than the others. It bullied its way to the front of the feed. Pigs were known to be mean at such times, and Nels wasn't about to enter and distribute the feed evenly for fear of being knocked off balance by the hungry stampede. While the pigs fed, he walked around to the back of their confinement.

An even more gruesome sight lay inside the pen. Remnants of a red plaid shirt, the only shirt he had ever seen Jake Bengtson wear, was trampled in the muddy tracks in the ground, and the body of Jake (he assumed) lay detached and partially buried. Only denim pant legs, arm bones, and the limp red shirt sleeves stuck out of the muck. The skull had been picked clean.

He cried aloud, "Oh my God! My God! What has happened here?" Running for his truck, he spotted Hans riding Buck up the driveway.

"What is that awful smell?" Hans shouted.

"What are you doing here? Shouldn't you be getting ready for school? Don't come any closer. Ride back home and tell Mom to call the sheriff and send him out here. He'll probably need a couple of deputies too. Mr. Bengtson is dead, and the pigs are starving. I'll stay here until the sheriff comes, and you get on to school. You hear me?"

"Yes, sir," said Hans, and raced away.

Nels's mind went back to the night before. *Oh Lord, what if Kinley had come and found this?*

Sheriff Barclay was there within fifteen minutes after receiving the call. He had brought with him an entourage of deputies, the county coroner, and animal control authorities. After Nels Swenson pointed the way to the dead body, they searched every inch of the Bengtson farm, looking for clues.

"What do you think, Sheriff?" Mr. Swenson asked.

Sheriff Barclay speculated. "It's all certainly suspicious, and I can't rule out foul play. Bengtson's truck is missing, the house is unlocked, and Mrs. Bengtson and their son haven't been around. But who would want to steal an old truck or kidnap someone from a run-down pig farm in rural Story County?"

"I too can only speculate on the cause of death at this point," said the coroner. "There's so little left of the victim to work with. The face of the victim is eaten away, the vital organs are no longer intact, and even most of the flesh is gone."

Several curious neighbors had followed the parade of officials who were at the scene.

"Look at old Boaris over there," said Mr. Johnson, pointing out the fattest pig. "I'd say he got more than his share of body parts."

"Yeah, he's a mean one," another neighbor added to the conversation.

Sheriff Barclay wrote as Nels and the other neighbors fed him bits of information. He also asked questions: "Does anyone know of any close relatives? Did the Bengtsons get along with the neighbors? Can you think of anyone who might know the whereabouts of the missus and the kid?"

"I don't," said Nels. "I do know Mrs. Bengtson doesn't drive. I suppose Bobby could though. He drove the tractor."

"I kind of remember that Mrs. Bengtson had relations in South Dakota. They came to visit once," offered another neighbor.

"Do you think that old truck could make it that far?" Nels asked.

The sheriff shouted to one of the deputies, "Check the registration on Bengtson's truck and put out an APB. It's a start."

Once the coroner had left with the remains and the dead pigs were hauled off, most of the crowd dispersed too. Nels Swenson came to the sheriff with a generous offer.

"Sheriff, there's enough feed in the barn for maybe a month. I'll come and feed the pigs until it's decided what to do with them, but I'm not set up to care for them at my farm."

Mr. Johnson, who also had lingered behind, said, "Maybe if Nels can fatten them up a bit, I might consider taking them. How about if I help feed them, say a couple of times a week, or Nels and I work something out between us?"

"Sounds like a plan, gentlemen. I appreciate any help you can offer," said the sheriff.

The remaining pigs had calmed down once their bellies were full. They were lolling in the muck now that the dead carcasses had been removed and hauled away.

Nels said to the sheriff, "If there's anything else I can do, let me know. Otherwise, I'll be going home."

"No," said the sheriff, "but I appreciate you checking the premises and your offer to care for the animals until their fate is decided. We'll be going through the house for a couple more hours looking for any clues to help find Mrs. Bengtson and the boy. Good day, sir."

"I'm leaving with a heavy heart, Sheriff, and I'll be careful what I say to my wife and kids. I don't want the boys starting rumors with their peers at school."

Sheriff Barclay had similar thoughts as he spoke to the media. "The body of a rural farmer was found this afternoon outside on his farm. The body was so decomposed that we can't be sure of the identity yet, and we may never know the cause of death. At this point, foul play is not suspected. Many of the animals on the farm were also found dead, from starvation."

"Did the deceased live alone and that's why no one found him before now?" asked one reporter.

"It appears he was living alone, but we are not able to give out names until his identity is confirmed and family is notified."

"What are officials doing to find his family? Are you sure there aren't any suspects in this mysterious death?"

"No, there are no suspects. We have an APB out on the only vehicle registered to the property owner, and we are currently trying to find connections," said Sheriff Barclay, choosing his words carefully. "I will keep the media updated as our investigation proceeds, but that is all I have for now."

"Can you give us more details on the location of the farm?" one interviewer persisted.

"No," Sheriff Barclay said, holding up his hands to indicate he was done with answering questions.

The questions continued as one of his deputies ushered the inquisitive media out of county headquarters.

"What kind of vehicle are you looking for? Car? Truck? Tractor?"

The deputy shut the door, leaving the media to speculate on their own.

The coroner called the next morning. "Well, Sheriff, I found no evidence or clues to determine what caused the death of the victim. Going by blood type and some of his dental work, I've identified the remains as those of Jake Bengtson, age forty-five, five feet ten inches tall. The cause of death will remain a mystery. There was not enough organ tissue to give me the whole story. I'm sorry."

"It's more than we knew yesterday. Good work under the circumstances," said the sheriff.

"I'll hang on to the remains until it's decided what to do with them."

"Hopefully that will be soon. Thanks, Doc."

The sheriff's deputy walked in with some news. "I think they've found Bengtson's truck just across the border in Omaha. The plates are missing, but make, model, condition, and color all point to Bengtson's vehicle. Another interesting thing: It had three bullet holes in it, one in the tire on the driver's side, one in the tailgate, and one that shattered the back window."

"Well, I'll be. Fill out the paperwork and bring the truck in so we can get started on the investigation."

"Already done, sir." The deputy waved the form and threw it on the sheriff's desk. "Also, sir, in the address book by the telephone at the Bengtsons' house, there were very few numbers listed, but two of them were out that direction: a Margaret Jones in Lincoln, Nebraska, and another listing in Colorado Springs, for William Smith."

"Great! This may be easier than we thought. Get on it," said the sheriff.

"Both are common names in highly populated areas, sir. It may take more time than you think. But Agnes is already making calls."

The sheriff shook his head. "Think I'll go have another look around the farm. I just hope we don't discover two more bodies."

The rifle resting inside the front door suddenly became an object of interest. Sheriff Barclay handled it carefully with gloved hands as he laid it in the back seat of the patrol car. *Perhaps Mr. Bengtson fired at an intruder stealing his truck.* He followed a trail of a possible escape route, starting at the front door where the gun rested and going down the path of the driveway to the street.

There were four empty chambers in the gun. He found three shell casings, two on the driveway and one in the street. The truck had three bullet holes; one shot may have missed. Hopefully, they'd find a bullet embedded somewhere in the truck to determine if it had come from this rifle. He already had Jake's, Bobby's, and Mrs.

Bengtson's fingerprints from the farm equipment and personal items in the house.

As Sheriff Barclay tromped through tall grass around the farm searching for evidence of freshly dug soil, more rotting flesh, or any stray animals, he abandoned the search the moment Nels Swenson pulled onto the property.

"Mr. Swenson," he called from the field as Nels came near.

"Hello, Sheriff."

"Here to feed the pigs?"

"Yeah."

"I noticed an empty chicken coop back there." He pointed toward the farm buildings. "What do you suppose happened to the chickens? I've been scanning the place and haven't run across any."

"Mrs. Bengtson kept a few for eggs and eating. I suppose they could have wandered off or were snatched by a fox if they weren't put inside after dark," Nels offered.

"Anyone around here the Bengtsons didn't get along with?"

"The boy was kind of ornery. He had several run-ins with my boys recently. In fact, it was the principal who sent me here to check on the Bengtsons because Bobby hadn't been to school for a couple of weeks and their phone had been disconnected. But basically, they kept to themselves and didn't neighbor much."

"How about the mister and missus? Did they get along?"

Nels hesitated, kicking around in the dirt at his feet. "I don't like to guess what goes on in another man's home, but the father was harsh with their boy, and the missus was overly protective of him. After a three-day suspension from school, Bobby showed up with multiple bruises, and the principal reported it to the authorities. Bobby never returned to school after that."

"This at the elementary school?"

"Yes," said Nels. "I talked to Principal Wheaton this morning before I came here. I hope that was okay. I didn't give him all the details. I just said it looked like Bobby and Mrs. Bengtson were gone and that Mr. Bengtson had died while tending the pigs at the farm."

"I appreciate that, sir," said the sheriff. "Well, I'll let you get to your business, Mr. Swenson. I think I'll go have a chat with Principal Wheaton. Good day."

Sheriff Barclay pulled into the elementary school parking lot an hour later with multiple questions on his mind. Inside, he spotted Principal Wheaton interacting with the kids in the hallway between morning classes.

The children cleared a path as the sheriff approached. He smiled at them and teased them until the bell rang, sending them off to class, which left him alone with Mr. Wheaton.

"I suppose you're here about the Bengtson boy, sir. I heard what happened from Nels Swenson this morning. Let's go into my office so we can talk."

"I need information concerning the family. It's a strange situation, Mr. Wheaton. From the boy's school records, is there a trusted family member, like a grandparent, aunt, or uncle, listed to contact in emergencies? Bobby and his mother seem to have disappeared and probably don't even know about Mr. Bengtson yet."

"Well, let me see," said the principal, leafing through the file cabinet. "Here's his information. It's a pretty thick folder. The kid's always in trouble. I've seen a pattern of injuries over time, and not all of Bobby's wounds this last time were caused by minor scrapes and fights here at school. But it's the first time I felt compelled to call child welfare authorities."

"What did they say? Did they visit the parents?"

"Yes. The letter from the social worker's visit is there on top," said Mr. Wheaton.

"It says here that Mr. Bengtson told them Bobby was kicked by a cow," the sheriff said. "I saw no evidence of cows on the property. It also says Mrs. Bengtson had visible bruises and contusions on her face and arms as well. How many days after your call did the social worker visit?"

"Actually, it was a truant officer who made the last visit. The date should be on there," said the principal. "Bobby's last day of school was two days after his suspension was lifted. That's the day I reported the nurse's findings and my own suspicions to the child welfare authorities. A truant officer made a visit the following day to talk with the parents. His follow-up visit took place two and a half weeks later, and there was no contact made at that time. That is when I called the Swenson's to see if they knew anything."

Sheriff Barclay had more questions for Mr. Wheaton. "Did the kid ever complain about his father?"

"No. And I only met the man once. He seemed nice and understanding the day he showed up to get Bobby after a ruckus with another student."

Looking over Bobby's registration information, the sheriff spotted the name Margaret Jones, one of the names found in Mrs. Bengtson's address book. He copied the number and address in case it differed from what they already had. Handing the folder back to Mr. Wheaton, he said, "I appreciate your time, sir. One more question. Given Bobby's records here, do you think the boy is capable of killing someone?"

"Oh my! That's a pretty loaded question, Sheriff. Uh, let me just say that I think Bobby is starved for attention. But killing someone? I doubt it. Surely you don't think Bobby is involved in his father's death. In spite of his behavior records, Bobby Bengtson was a very likable kid."

CHAPTER 13

The day Jake Bengtson had been found dead, Mario heard Hans tell the bus driver and all the kids on the bus that Bobby's dad and the pigs were dead. By day's end the story became more enhanced. Mario listened to morbid tales the kids shared on the bus ride coming home. Someone had heard it from someone who was there and saw the grisly body; somebody else knew somebody who worked at county headquarters, who said pigs had eaten Bobby's dad.

Mario, Hans, and Lupita came home with all the disturbing details.

"Bobby's dad was eaten by the pigs, and all that was left were his feet, skull, and ribs," said Lupita, running to tell Mario's grandma, who was working in the garden.

"What?!" Grandma said.

"That's probably why Dad didn't want me on the property when I rode up there," Hans said. "It had to be something really nasty like that."

His mother offered a reasonable explanation: "The body was outside and badly decomposed, and many of the pigs had starved to death. That's why he didn't want you there, Hans."

"That's true. The stink was horrid. Dead pigs, pig crap—I've never smelled anything so bad."

"I think the pigs ate all of Bobby and his mother, and that's why the authorities can't find them," said Lupita innocently.

Mario gave them his theory on the situation: "I think Bobby

killed his dad and threw him into the pigpen, and his mother is hiding him so he doesn't get put in juvie hall."

"I like that. It makes sense. I could see Bobby doing it," Hans said.

Mario's grandma covered her ears. "For crying out loud! Stop all this gibberish. We'll know the answer when they find them. Now, there are snacks in the fridge and a list of chores for you boys on the table. Go get busy. And no more talk about the Bengtsons."

"Yes, ma'am," they said in unison, and hurried off.

A month had gone by. There were no new leads in the Bengtson case. Sheriff Barclay had run into nothing but dead ends with the little information he had gathered. Margaret Jones and William Smith might as well have been phantom names in a fantasy world. The number for Margaret had been disconnected several years ago, and her address was now under another name. One of the many William Smiths recalled selling Jake Bengtson a truck four or five years earlier but said he had had no personal relationship with him.

The only thing Sheriff Barclay did know for sure was that the shots fired into the truck had come from the rifle found in the house. One bullet had lodged in the rear tire, causing a slow leak, which was probably the reason the truck had been abandoned—that and the fact that it also had run out of gas. The lone bullet matched the caliber of the shell casings left along the drive and in the road.

The three different fingerprints on the gun matched those of two family members. Most of them were Jake's, on the stock and trigger, and one set belonged to Bobby. Apparently, Bobby had picked it up or used it at some point.

But the mystery focused on the third set of prints on the gun barrel. Virginia Bengtson was ruled out when the prints on her personal hand mirror and on the hand mixer in the kitchen proved not to match the ones on the barrel.

The questionable prints were also found on the doorknob and the doorframe, but none were on the truck. There wasn't really a crime scene yet, only a missing persons investigation. The unknown prints, the sheriff sent to the state laboratory, hoping for identification. He knew that in the time it would take to process the prints, the case might already be solved.

Nels came to the Bengtson farm to feed the pigs one morning only to find a rig loading up pigs. "Someone buy the pigs?" he hollered to the drivers.

"No, the county had a couple of offers, but I have orders to pick them up and haul them to the rendering plant on the south side of Des Moines. Some pigs tested positive for swine dysentery, one of the most expensive diseases to eradicate if it spreads through the herd," said one of the drivers. "They wouldn't be fit to eat or sell."

Nels smiled. "Can't say I'm sorry or that I'll miss them. Winter is on its way, and coming here each day is getting tiresome."

"You must be the guy who's been feeding them. It was nice of you to fatten them up to be made into by-products," the driver said, chuckling.

"Yeah. I was about to start complaining." Nels laughed. "Besides, their feed was running out. There's probably another two days' worth left in the barn."

"What kind of farm do you operate?" asked the other driver.

"Corn, soybeans, a herd of beef, and quite a few dairy cows. Glad to see these squealers go. Now I can concentrate on getting my crops in."

"Good luck to you, sir," the main driver said, hoisting himself into the cab of the semi.

The other fellow secured the gate on the pigpen and locked the trailer door. He had barely seated himself in the cab as the semi pulled away with the pigs squealing as if already being slaughtered.

Nels could still hear them a mile away as he walked around the place, checking the barn and hanging Bengtson's tools inside before leaving. A slight rustle in the corner caught his attention. He grabbed a shovel, expecting a bull snake or a rat in the hay next to the corncrib. Two calico kittens wandered out to where he was standing, aimed to strike.

"Well, look here," he said, throwing the shovel aside and gently picking up the kittens. "You two I have room for at my farm. Do you have a mama, or are you orphans?" As he cuddled them, he looked around. There had not been any cats on the property since he'd been coming, and he suspected they had recently been dumped by city folks.

"Two more mouths to feed," Kinley remarked as she took possession of the kittens Nels handed her upon his return home.

"Plenty of milk here and all the mice they can stomach," Nels said. "One cat for each boy."

"Did these come from the Bengtsons'?" Kinley asked.

"Yep. And the pigs are gone. They were hauling them off when I showed up this morning."

She paused then asked, "What will happen to the place now?"

"The bank will probably foreclose on it. They've lived there less than six years, and I doubt the place has been paid off. Mrs. Bengtson and the boy may show up before all that takes place. It's a lot of paperwork and red tape to repossess an estate."

"An estate? Really, Nels, it's more of an eyesore than an estate. Even if the police find them, Mrs. Bengtson won't be able to stay there without help or income," Kinley said sadly.

"I know, dear. We'll have to wait and see what happens."

Poor Mrs. Bengtson and Bobby. God rest their souls, wherever they are.

Nels gave Kinley a tender embrace as Henry and Tommy stopped at the end of the driveway with a tractor, a wagon, and a corn picker, ready for work.

"We just finished the corn on my back acres," shouted Tommy. "Do you want to start on the field along the river?"

"I'd rather work on the acres next to the road first. It'll bring a better yield while the weather cooperates. Half the crop along the river didn't develop to full capacity because of spring flooding. It'll be last on my list. That's what we'll use to feed the livestock," Nels replied to his stepson.

"Understand," said Tommy. "Do you think we should try to salvage what's left of Bengtson's crops? At least enough to feed the pigs awhile longer?"

"No need to worry about that. They hauled the pigs away this morning," Nels said, climbing in the tractor cab with Henry.

"Good," said Tommy.

"About time," Henry added. "One less thing to worry about. Now we can concentrate on the harvest."

"How long will you stay this year, Henry?" Nels asked, settling in beside him.

"We'll be here until the crops are in and the equipment is cleaned and put away. Lupita wants to stay in school until Christmas break."

"That sounds like a good plan, Henry."

"The girl doesn't want to go home at all, but we have family to care for in Brownsville. And Carmen doesn't like the freezing Midwest winters. I will be back again come spring."

Nels asked, "Does Lupita go to school during that time?"

Henry smiled. "Oh yes. She never misses. She wants to be an animal doctor someday."

"Fantastic. When that day comes and you're still around, I'd be glad to help her achieve her dream."

"You are too kind, sir."

"Lupita is like family to us. You all are."

Supper was cold when the men returned from the fields. Kinley set to warming a plate for Nels.

"Sheriff Barclay called twice this afternoon," she said. "You're to call him back in the morning."

"What does he want now?"

"He wouldn't say, but he sounded serious."

"Well, I can't be bothered with the Bengtson farm anymore. I've got my own business to take care of before winter."

"I'm curious too, Nels. Maybe he's just looking for more information."

Nels thought for a moment, then said, "I've got a wagonload of corn we didn't get to the co-op today. I plan to be first in line in the morning. I'll stop by his office after I've unloaded."

Nels stepped inside county headquarters the next day after his delivery to the co-op.

Sheriff Barclay stood. As he led Nels into an interrogation room down the hall from his office, he said solemnly, "We need somewhere we can talk privately."

"You're scaring me, sir. What's wrong?"

"Explain to me how your fingerprints got on Bengtson's rifle."

CHAPTER 14

The question posed by the sheriff stunned Nels. It was beyond what he expected. "What a question, sir. My prints were on that rifle because the morning I went to check on the Bengtsons, the gun was resting inside the front door and I knocked it over accidently when I stepped inside. I picked it up by the barrel and set it back in place."

"So far, so good," said Sheriff Barclay. "The state forensics lab determined your prints were on the barrel. Unless you've forgotten, the state keeps prints of suspects and felons in a database."

Nels replied, "I understand. It's because I was a suspect in my first wife's death."

"And incarcerated for concealing the body of your brother-in-law, Homer Speers, failing to report his death, and other charges related to that investigation," Sheriff Barclay added.

"Sheriff, that's all in the past, and you know the story. Now you're trying to connect me with foul play in what happened to Jake. The things I did years ago were done to protect the women at Swenson Farms. I served eighteen months, and I paid all the fines connected to Homer's case."

"Nels, I'm just looking at all the possibilities."

"Jake and I got along fine. What motive would I have to hurt Jake or his family? He treated my wife and me like good neighbors. We didn't socialize, but there was respect between us." There was a pause before he added, "So, you think Jake was killed?"

The sheriff leaned closer to him in a confidential manner. "Four shell casings were fired from that rifle. Three of them hit the back of Bengtson's truck. Only three sets of prints were found on the gun: yours, Jakes, and young Bobby's.

"You don't say? What went on at that farm? Any theories, sir?"

"I was hoping you'd help me out, Nels. Whatever it was, it happened shortly after the visit by Child Protection Services."

Nels felt sick to his stomach. His head fell into his hands as he muttered, "Mr. Bengtson probably wasn't happy with authorities questioning him about Bobby's injuries. He had a short wick when it came to the kid. I'm getting an awful feeling about what he might have done to Bobby—or the missus if she tried to protect the boy from punishment."

"So, it's a possibility young Bengtson shot his father trying to protect himself or his mother? Maybe buried him in the pigpen and left?"

"Oh my God," said Nels. "How gruesome. My mind can't even go there. Bobby's an ornery kid, but ...." His voice faltered; he couldn't finish the thought.

"We need to find him and his mother," said the sheriff. He reached over and patted Nels on the shoulder. "If for no other reason than to know who did what, how, and why. You're free to go. Nothing personal in regard to asking about the rifle. I know where your heart lies from those previous cases. You seem to have a sense of vigilantism when it comes to protecting the innocent and downtrodden. I wanted to make sure it hadn't happened again with Bobby and Mrs. Bengtson."

"Thank you, Sheriff. I'll do everything I can to help you find them."

Nels headed straight to the fields, where Henry and Tommy were already at work. He did so deliberately to avoid being quizzed by Kinley. He needed time to think and digest the sheriff's latest findings before sharing them with her.

"About time you got here with the other wagon," yelled Tommy.

"I had an errand to attend to in town," Nels responded.

"It's Henry's turn to take his load to be weighed and credited. Are you ready to fill up another wagon, Pops?"

"Yep! Let's do it."

Between him and Henry, they hauled six loads of corn to the co-op before quitting time, and a seventh load was ready for early the next day.

After they sat down for the evening meal, Kinley started to ask about Nels's day. "Well, are you going to tell me what happened in town with the …?"

Nels stopped her with his eyes, looking toward the boys, an indication that the subject of the sheriff was off-limits at the table.

"Yes. We had a very profitable day," he said. "The price of corn was up for the early harvest, and we should be able to get that same amount again tomorrow after harvesting the north property. Tommy's soybeans need another week or so. Everything's working out fine."

Kinley gave Nels a curious look. "Anything else I should know?"

While Hans shoveled down his supper, Mario played with his food.

"What's wrong, Mario?" Nels asked his grandson.

"I was wondering if the sheriff had any news about Bobby and his mother. I know he called yesterday."

"Oh, that," Nels said, planning to skirt the issue. "I did happen to see the sheriff. He asked if we would have time to harvest Bengtson's hay and use it for our animals since I'd helped them out so much. I said I didn't want it but that Mr. Johnson down the road might. I'm sorry to say there is nothing new to report about Bobby and his mom."

"I wonder if he even knows his dad is dead," Mario mused, continuing to pursue the issue.

Hans reached for another helping of mashed potatoes. "I'd say no, or else they would be here to bury him. If they're somewhere up north or out west, they wouldn't hear any news of an Iowa farmer found dead on his land. That's only news here in Story County."

Kinley smiled. "Good point, Hans. That's the most sense I've heard from you on the subject."

Mario didn't give up. "If they were just visiting someone, they should have been back a long time ago. Bobby needs to be in school."

"The dinner table is not the place to have troublesome conversation. Can we just eat in peace?" Nels said with irritation in his voice. "I'm really tired after today. Think I'll turn in early after I key in our stats from the co-op."

"Grandpa, I can do that," Mario offered.

Nels thought for a moment. "I'll let you do that. They need to be done each day for fear I'll forget, lose them, or end up with too many entries, which would cause me to make more mistakes. They're on the desk next to the computer. Make me proud, boy."

Nels headed upstairs and was asleep before Kinley came to bed.

The next morning, Nels, hearing the corn picker out front, swigged down his coffee and rushed outside. Hopping on Tommy's tractor, which was attached to an empty wagon, he was ready to start the day.

The boys, after grabbing their lunches, ran, climbed on the back of the tractor, and called to Lupita. She was out of breath as she jumped in the cab with Nels.

"Buenos días, Senorita Morales," Nels said to her in a jolly voice. "Where can I take you this morning?"

"Oh, Senor Nels, you are so funny. The bus is already waiting for us. Step on it." Her laughter exaggerated the dimple in her right cheek, and the beautiful dark eyes in her small oval face danced with merriment.

"At your service, madam." He shouted to the back of the tractor, "Hang on, boys."

Henry drove Nels's truck with another wagon laden with corn from the previous day and followed the parade down the long driveway. Tommy, in the corn picker cab, turned south at the end of the driveway, heading for the forty acres across from Bengtson's place. Nels waited until the bus pulled away with the children, then followed Tommy. Henry went north toward town with the load of corn.

As Nels passed the Bengtson farm, he recognized neighbor Johnson's red Farmall tractor mowing Bengtson's hayfield. Nels removed his straw hat and waved it out the window at Johnson.

Two hours later, Henry returned from town with the empty wagon. "I'm sorry to be late, Nels, but the line was very long at the grain elevator."

"Well, it's expected at this time of year, especially when the weather is so right for picking. Would you want to take the next load in, or would you prefer I do it?"

Henry paused before answering. "Maybe you would get a better price. I think the farmer ahead of me got five cents more a bushel than we did."

"Really?!" Nels raised his voice. "Are you telling me they discriminated against you?"

"I don't know why. The man also took two farmers behind me in line ahead of me."

"You stay here and work with Tommy and let me take the next load."

"Sí. I do not want any trouble."

Nels was on his way to the grain elevator when Kinley drove in the field gate. He waited as she got out of the Jeep and removed a wicker basket from the front seat. "I hope that's the fried chicken we had left over from last night."

"You got it, babe. Even made some fresh biscuits and a fruit salad."

"I'm going into town right now. If you can leave me some in the cooler over there under the tree, I'll have mine when I get back."

"If you wait until I get these to Tommy and Henry, then I'll go with you. It'll give us time to talk," she said.

"Okay, what's the big secret with Sheriff Barclay?" Kinley asked once she and Nels were on the road.

"Something terribly dramatic must have taken place at Bengtson's farm. Barclay found that four shots had recently been fired from Jake's rifle, and three of them left holes in the back of Jake's truck. I've thought it over a hundred times in my mind and can't come up with a logical explanation. I didn't want the boys to hear about it," he said, avoiding telling her the part about his finger prints on the gun.

"Oh no. I'm glad you didn't. Mario seems to be carrying around a lot of guilt. He's thinking he may be the cause of their disappearance."

"I think some of it hinges on how he feels about losing his own father. The emotions are still fresh in his mind," he replied.

"You're right. He's a sensitive boy with such a big heart."

They drove on in silence before Kinley asked, "Doesn't Henry usually take the grain into town?"

"That's another thing," Nels said with a long sigh. "The co-op gave Henry a bad time this morning. He thinks they gave him less money than the others got, and the fellow in charge unloaded two farmers behind him in line first. That had better not be the case."

"That's hard to believe," said Kinley. "Henry has been with us for three seasons. Why single him out now?"

"I don't know. I hope it's all a misunderstanding. We'll find out soon," he said, pulling in line at the grain elevator.

It was a forty-minute wait before they reached the front of the lineup. Halfway through, Nels took an empty gas can and walked across the street to a gas station. He had forgotten to check the fuel gauge before pulling in. The constant stopping and starting had sucked away what little gas he had.

"What's the going rate this morning, sir?" Nels asked when it was his turn up front.

"Two fifty-seven per bushel," said the fellow.

"Has it changed since early morning?" he asked.

"No, sir."

"Then please check a previous load on my account this morning, sir."

"Right now?" the man asked, looking at the trucks and wagons behind Nels's vehicle.

"Now!" Nels answered sternly. "The name is Nels Swenson. If it shows the price is different, see that it gets corrected before I leave."

"Yes, sir, Mr. Swenson. Please pull ahead so they can start unloading. Check with the office when you're done."

Kinley waited in the truck while he stepped inside the office.

"Was there a discrepancy on my account?" Nels asked the clerk on duty.

"Yes, there was a price difference. An honest mistake, I'm sure," the clerk said.

"How much difference?"

"Five cents per bushel. Whoever filled out the form made the seven to look like a two. Sorry about that, sir. The correction has been made. Here is the paperwork for your records."

Nels thought for a second before deciding to pursue the matter further. "If the price for corn is two fifty-seven at the start of the day, why wouldn't someone question why one person was given two fifty-two? And another thing: My worker Henry Morales said others were directed to pull around him and were taken ahead of him in line."

"Oh, I'm sure that didn't happen, Mr. Swenson, unless there is a reasonable explanation."

"Mr. Morales is a good man, a hardworking man, and very smart. I hope it wasn't a matter of discrimination. I will be keeping a close watch from now on. I will also bring this matter to the attention of the grange at our next meeting to see if other farmers have experienced similar 'misunderstandings,'" he said, using air quotes to make his point.

"I'm sure that won't be necessary, Mr. Swenson. I'll see that the supervisor and the manager are made aware of your complaint," she said.

"Nothing personal, ma'am. I know you're just doing your job, but I will pursue the matter just to keep things on the up and up."

CHAPTER 15

The harvest was in, and there was much to give thanks for at Thanksgiving. Nels reached across the table and handed Henry a generous check.

"No, Nels. This is too much," Henry said. "There is still work to do, and we will not pull away until school is out for Christmas. What if I can't finish my job?"

"I've taken everything into account. We had a bountiful year, and you deserve every penny."

"Gracias," he said with a modest bow of his head.

"We hope to see you again in the spring," said Kinley.

Carmen Morales blushed. "I will not be returning next year with my husband. Our baby will be born in April, and I will remain with my family in Texas before and after the birth."

Kinley grasped her hand. "Oh, Carmen, I am so happy for you. How could you keep this news from me?"

"I wanted to be sure. It has been over twelve years since Lupita was born. It was a surprise to us too."

"Maybe I will get a son," said Henry.

"Or another beautiful girl like Lupita," Nels interjected.

A little grin graced Henry's face as he looked at his daughter. "That will be fine too. I do make pretty girls."

The laughter around the table caused Lupita to redden. "Papa!" she said, hiding her face in her hands.

Mario, the only one who didn't join in the merriment, added, "Will Lupita come back with you, Senor Henry?"

"I will come back, but I think Lupita should stay and help her mother," Henry answered.

There was a slight groan from Mario's side of the table. Nels saw the disappointment written on his grandson's face.

Nels directed his next question to Henry: "Will the baby come while you are here, Henry?"

Henry sighed. "It will be a close call, but probably yes. The work is important for us to pay bills and help other family members."

"We can work something out when the time comes, Henry. I've got some good help right here to fill in until you get back," Nels said, staring at Hans and Mario. "You take the time you need. You can't miss such an event."

"Aw, Dad, I thought I'd try out for baseball next year," Hans moaned.

"Like I said, we'll figure it out."

Kinley and Carmen pushed away from the table, each taking a stack of dishes with them to the kitchen. They returned seconds later with dessert: pumpkin pie, date cake, and a large bowl of whipped cream.

Mario had grown very quiet. He picked at the luscious dessert. Nels knew his grandson was about to suffer yet another loss, namely, his closest companion Lupita.

Mario hung close to Lupita during their last days before winter break. He watched as Senor Henry began loading their personal belongings into their old truck. One day of school remained.

He hoped Lupita would like the present he had secretly worked on in the basement after chores were done. Grandpa had given him some scrap wood and nails and had been his consultant for the project.

Hans, anxious to start Christmas vacation, leaped off the school bus, hooting and hollering, and ran toward the barn. "Me and Buck are going for a ride before the storm hits. You guys coming?"

"No," said Lupita, picking up one of the calico kittens on her way up the driveway. "Papa will want to leave soon if there is a storm coming."

"Not now. Maybe later," Mario said to Hans. He nonchalantly took Lupita's hand as they slowly walked toward the house.

"I will miss you, Mario," Lupita said shyly, looking away and nuzzling the kitten.

"I've got something for you," he said as they came to the porch steps. He let go of her hand. "Wait here."

She sat on the steps with the kitten asleep in her arms.

Mario came back carrying a large, roughly wrapped cardboard box with a regifted red bow.

"Oh, Mario, I'm sorry I didn't get you anything for Christmas." The kitten landed on the steps as Lupita stood to accept the present. Excitement was written on her face and in her actions as she ripped off the lid.

"It's not necessarily a Christmas present but something to remember us by. I made it myself."

The excitement came to a halt as she stared in the box. "What is it?" she said with a let-down expression, lifting the item out of the box.

"It's a flower box. And the envelope inside it is filled with seeds and bulbs from Grandma's garden—all the red flowers you like. You can plant them in the box when you get back to Texas."

"That is so sweet, Mario. I love it. I will remember Swenson farm every time they bloom. Thank you for such a nice gift."

He had hoped, almost expected, her to throw her arms around him and give him his first kiss, but it didn't happen. For one thing, the moment was interrupted by Hans riding up on Buck. *I wonder if she even likes my gift. Or is she just being polite by saying all those things?*

"Are you sure you won't change your mind about taking a ride, Lupita?" Hans said with a grin.

She ran down the porch steps. He grabbed her hand and pulled her up behind him. Her arms instantly went around his waist as he spurred Buck to a trot.

Mario stared after them, listening to their laughter as they galloped off. The gift he had worked so hard on was abandoned on the porch. *Let the storm blow it away or the snow bury it. See if I care.*

He ran to the barn and beat the snot out of the speed bag while tears clouded his eyes.

The next morning from, his upstairs bedroom window, Mario saw Hans give Lupita the calico kitten before the Moraleses pulled away. Lupita nuzzled Kitty and blew Hans a kiss, which he pretended to catch.

Good riddance. It was then that Mario noticed his special gift to Lupita was also gone from the porch.

CHAPTER 16

It was a new year, January 1994. School was back in session after the holiday break, but Mario still missed the company of his best friend Lupita. She could always be counted on for a game of checkers, Sorry, or Monopoly late in the afternoon. The two of them were a good match, equal competitors, often talking over and sharing their mistakes and strategies.

Hans wasn't a game player unless it involved sports or physical competition. Except for boxing, Mario felt he could never win or even come close to a victory against Hans. Besides, he had not forgiven him for stealing Lupita's attention on her last day at the farm—maybe even forever.

At dusk one evening, Mario decided to take Windy for ride. The fields were layered in a mix of snow and mud, so he stuck to the road. The air was nippy but brisk. Darkness would likely set in before his return home. As he passed the Bengtson place, he noticed an occasional puff of smoke coming out of the chimney. Whatever was burning smelled good, like Grandpa Fontanini's pipe, and added a sweet fragrance to the cold air that stung his nostrils. His guess was cedar or cypress firewood.

He ventured up the driveway. *Maybe I should go home and tell Grandpa and Grandma before I go any farther.*

But his curiosity begged him to investigate.

Tethering Windy to a porch rail, he quietly went up the steps and looked in through the front window. A flicker of light, coming from a candle burning in the middle of a table at the back of the house, could be seen through the dining room door.

Mario shielded his eyes with his hands as he squinted for a clearer look inside. Windy gave a loud whinny. A silhouetted figure instantly blew out the candle.

Mario got only a glimpse of the shadow as it moved impulsively, quick to put out the light, but the outline was definitely that of Bobby. The shaft of hair Bobby always flipped out of his eyes, the skinny long arms, and the height of the figure left Mario to conclude that it couldn't have been anyone else. *Why would he and his mother try to hide if they were back?*

"Bobby! Open up! It's me, Mario."

Silence filled the air. Mario knocked and shouted again. "Bobby! Mrs. Bengtson! Open up. I'm glad you're home. We were worried about you."

The door opened a crack, and Bobby peeked out. His eyes darted around the space on the porch and then at the driveway. "Are you by yourself?"

"Yes."

"Where is my father? And the pigs?"

"You don't know?"

"How would I? I've been gone."

Mario hesitated. "I'm not sure how to tell you, Bobby, so I'll just say it. Your father is dead. They found him outside. Many of the pigs had starved, and the ones that survived were hauled away, too sick to recover."

There was now a mixture of fear and confusion in Bobby's eyes, but a lack of tears. "Dead, huh? Gone? All of them? How did he die? I'd really like to know how he died."

Mario wanted to choose his words carefully. It would be insensitive to blurt out that Bobby's father had been eaten by the pigs. "I don't think they know yet, Bobby. The sheriff has been trying to find you and your mother. I will go home and have Grandpa call him. He'll tell you everything that's been going on here with the farm and the investigation into your father's death."

"No! You can't do that, Mario."

"Why not?"

"Because my mother is dead too, and I've run away."

"Run away from where?"

"From my aunt and uncle in South Dakota. You can't tell anyone. I don't want to end up in juvie prison or a foster home. I'm begging you, Mario, please don't tell. I'm fine here. There is plenty of food in the cellar, and I can find enough wood for the stove."

"Why do you think they would put you in juvie prison? Someone is bound to find out you're here, Bobby. I saw and smelled the smoke coming from the chimney."

"I'll just be more careful and not burn any more logs until after dark."

Mario started to ask Bobby about what had happened to his mother, when headlights turned into the driveway from the road.

"Please don't give me away, Mario." With that, Bobby disappeared into the darkened house.

"Mario, what are you doing here at the Bengtsons' place?" his grandpa asked.

"I was riding home and thought I smelled smoke." He looked up, but there was no evidence of smoke coming out the chimney. *Bobby must have doused the fire.*

"Your grandma and I started to worry about you. I spotted Windy's tracks headed up here," Nels said, sniffing the air. "I do smell something."

"Yeah, I checked around the place, but it must be coming from somewhere else," Mario lied.

"Well, get along home, boy." Nels turned the truck around. Mario followed on Windy.

How long can I keep this from Grandpa and Grandma? Mrs. Bengtson is dead, huh? I wonder what happened to her? I'll check with

Bobby again tomorrow. That makes him an orphan like me. I won't say anything until I know more.

"Those are some rosy cheeks you've got there," Mario's grandma greeted as he walked in the door. "Why were you gone so long?"

"I just lost track of time," he replied.

"There's one piece of apple pie left," Hans said. "You want to arm wrestle for it?"

"You can have it. I'm going to my room."

"Aw, you're no fun," said Hans.

"You'd win it anyway."

"Something wrong, dear?" Mario's grandma asked.

"No. I'm tired. I'm going to my room to listen to records and try to figure out a project for 4-H."

"Okay. Are you sure you don't want to take a snack with you?"

"No. I'm good."

Kinley sat down with Hans at the table and waited for Nels to put the truck away. Five minutes later, Nels came in, carrying the two bottles of milk she had asked him earlier to bring in from the dairy.

"Where'd you find Mario?" Kinley asked.

"At Bengtson's place."

"Doing what?"

"Said he smelled smoke, so he checked around the house and barn."

"I swear," she said, "he is going to mourn that boy and his mother until they're found. How long has it been now, four or five months?"

"It was last October," said Hans. "I say good riddance. I don't miss Bobby, and I hope he never comes back."

"Go wash up for supper," Kinley said, ignoring his remarks.

"By the way, Kinley, did you fill an order from the dairy this morning?" Nels asked.

"No. Why? The last order was two days ago," she said.

"I thought the inventory looked a little short, is all," he replied.

Mario found it hard to concentrate in school the next day. Anxious to hear Bobby's story, he planned to take another ride after school and after his chores were done. *I'll wait until Hans is occupied before riding off. Otherwise, he will follow along. It's my secret about Bobby for now.*

The class was laughing as Mario looked up from his book, somewhat startled, to see Miss Henderson, the math teacher, standing next to his desk with her arms crossed over her chest.

"Oh, sorry, Miss Henderson."

"Mario, please go to the blackboard and do the next problem," she said.

"What number is it again?"

"Page twenty-one, problem nine."

He fished his math book from the bottom of the pile of books in front of him. "Yes, ma'am."

The last bell of the day rang as he wrote the answer on the board. The teacher dismissed the class, and Mario ran and got on the bus.

Hans scooted into the seat beside him. "Where were you today? The teacher called your name twice. Were you sleeping with your eyes wide open behind that blank look?"

"No. I had things on my mind."

"Like what?"

"Just things."

"Are you still mourning Lupita?"

"No. Why would you say that?"

"Just wondered. You've been all moony-eyed since she left," Hans said sarcastically.

"So what if I am? She's my best friend, and I do miss her. Who is your best friend, Hans?"

"I thought you were," said Hans. "We kind of look out for each other. That's what best friends do, right?"

"Yeah, I guess. Do you think anybody misses Bobby? Did he even have any friends?"

Hans stood up. "Who cares? If you're going to be so woeful, I'm going to sit somewhere else."

"Fine," said Mario as Hans moved to the front of the bus. *That should keep him away from me for the rest of the day.*

"Grandma, I think I'll take a ride before supper—unless you have something for me to do," Mario said.

"Okay, but be back here in an hour. Supper is ready to put on the table when your grandpa comes home."

"I promise I'll be back."

When his grandmother left and went into the laundry room, Mario grabbed two slices of homemade bread from the middle of the loaf and put a fried chicken breast in a plastic bag.

As Mario was saddling Windy, Hans came into the barn. "Where you headed?"

"Just taking a ride to clear my head. I kind of want to be alone to think."

"No problem here. I've had enough of your thoughts for one day," Hans replied.

Good.

Half an hour later, Mario was in Bobby's backyard, tethering Windy to the clothesline pole and rapping on the door.

Bobby answered, wearing a parka with a blanket wrapped around him. "It's dang cold in here," he said to Mario. "I'm afraid to start a fire until after dark."

"Here, I brought you some food." Mario handed him the plastic sack. The furniture in the living room was covered with sheets, and what wasn't covered was thick with dust.

"I've got plenty of food, but no meat or bread. Could use some milk too. Kind of tired of canned fruits and vegetables," Bobby said while wolfing down the provisions Mario had brought.

"How long have you been living like this? Doesn't anyone ever come around?" It was obvious Bobby wasn't showering or taking out the garbage. Both smelled quite ripe.

"I've been here about two weeks. A couple of guys came last week and I hid in the basement. I heard them talking about getting the place ready for an auction come spring."

"Then what will you do?"

"I don't know," he said sadly. "I'll figure it out when the time comes. One guy said they should at least keep the water on so the pipes don't freeze and bust. But there's no electric or gas."

"Why don't you come home with me? Grandpa will know what to do. He'll do the right thing for you."

"I can't take the chance. After my mom died, I didn't want to stay in South Dakota. My aunt is nice, but my uncle's mean—mean as my dad. So, I figured that if I was going to live with mean, it might as well be back in Iowa. I hiked and rode whenever I could get a ride this direction. Besides, my dad needed to know what he did to Mom. He killed her. I hope his death was gruesome."

"Bobby!" Mario couldn't believe he and Bobby were able to talk to each other about such private feelings. "Why do you say he killed her?"

"It's a long story. Short version: One of the bullets he fired at us when we left hit her."

Mario looked at his watch. He barely had enough time to get home. "I want to hear more, but I promised Grandma I'd be home for supper. She'll start to get suspicious if I'm late. I'll be back tomorrow."

He thought there were tears in Bobby's eyes as he started to leave.

"Thanks for not ratting me out, Mario."

CHAPTER 17

The following morning, Mario awoke to deep snow from an overnight blizzard, which was still raging. The temperature had dropped drastically, visibility was zero, and snowdrifts filled the ditches and low-lying areas surrounding the farm. Since the roads were impassable, school had been canceled.

Mario and Hans ran outside, hurried through their chores, and quickly returned to the house. They brought with them warm eggs from beneath the feathers of sitting hens, and fresh milk from the cooler of the Swenson dairy, slopping some in bowls for the barn cats as they ran.

Mario, watching from inside the warm kitchen as the cats devoured their meal within the shelter of the porch before it froze, thought of Bobby. There was plenty of milk to share but no way to get it to him. *I hope he starts a fire today. No one will be out in this weather to see or question his smoking chimney. Is it time for me to tell Grandpa about Bobby? I can't bear the thought of finding him frozen or starved to death.*

Mario was still pondering this in late afternoon. When the winds died down, he saw from his upstairs window a wisp of smoke in the direction of Bobby's place, and felt better.

Before he put the binoculars away, he spotted someone slipping through their barnyard carrying a knapsack. Mario focused in on the figure as it climbed over their fence behind the dairy barn and then crawled through the snowy trees leading to the road.

"Oh, Bobby, you fool." He continued watching the road as Bobby sank and pulled himself out of one drift after another on his way back home until he was out of sight. The holes he left behind in the snow were quickly filled as the wind whipped more snow across the flatland, making them invisible again.

Grandpa was sitting down and staring at the computer screen at the foot of the stairs as Mario came down from his room.

"What do you think, Mario? We did so well last year. Should we use the same crops this year?"

"The nice thing about this DOS system is that it can total the prices from '93 and you can compare them to the year before. Here, let me show you." Leaning over Grandpa's shoulder, Mario highlighted the soy column and pushed a button, and the figures were totaled in the bottom cell. "Now let's look at the year before. See! Beans went up three times more in price. So, maybe you should put in more beans this year," he concluded.

"God, I love this new technology." Grandpa chuckled. "Show me again how you did that. The monthly grange meeting is at the end of the week. I'll feel out the other members on the subject of soybeans, if I'm able to get there. Dang weather," he said, glancing out the window.

"If you want, Grandpa, we can rake off the totals for the last five years so you can show them the changes."

"No. They will already know from farm reports and using their old-fashioned ways, but Swenson Farms is a state-of-the-art operation. If I give away my intentions by flashing those figures around at the grange, you know what that means."

"Yeah, less money per bushel if everyone plants soybeans," said Mario.

"How did you get so smart? Right now, I'm going to follow my nose into the kitchen."

Kinley pulled three loaves of bread from the oven. The warmth and aroma of fresh bread and ginger cookies made the kitchen a popular place. Hans came from his room, sniffing and sucking in the fragrant air. Nels poured a cup of coffee and sat at the table, waiting for the cookies. The boys followed his lead with glasses of milk.

Mario's perception of the cozy scene made him feel loved, wanted, and grateful to be part of a family. Once again, his mind wandered back to Bobby's situation. "I hope wherever Bobby is, he will be happy and safe. Maybe one day he can have a good home." The statement came out of nowhere, a shock both to him and the other family members.

"Are you on that 'feel sorry for Bobby' kick again?" Hans said with annoyance.

"I guess I am. Thank you, Grandpa and Grandma, for giving me a home and all the love that goes with it."

"We wouldn't have it any other way," said his grandma, kissing his forehead as she placed the cookies on the table.

"Let me accompany you on my little violin," said Hans, pretending to play an imaginary instrument. "Is there another verse?" He continued to drag the fantasy bow across imaginary strings while he pantomimed fingering keys.

"Knock it off, Hans," Mario said. He felt a rush of anger increasing his pulse as a flush of color crept toward his face. "I just hope you never have to go without food, a warm bed, or parents." He grabbed two cookies and headed back upstairs.

"Geez!" Hans said after Mario had left. "I was just funning him. Why is he so touchy about Bobby all of a sudden? It's like that's all he thinks about."

"I don't know, dear," said Kinley. "I'm not sure what's going on with him."

Nels stopped his wife from running upstairs after Mario. "For all we know, Bobby and his mother are better off where they are. Neither of them had much of a life with Jake."

The community center in Ames was packed with farmers from the surrounding area for the grange meeting. It was Friday night.

Sheriff Barclay greeted Nels and Tommy at the door as they kicked the snow off their boots. "I see you survived the blizzard. Everything okay at Swenson Farms?"

"Yes, sir." Tommy nodded, unwrapping his muffler and removing his earmuffs. "Pretty good crowd considering the weather, Sheriff."

"Yep. All's safe and sound," Nels said, shaking hands with him.

"Nels, can I speak with you in private for a second?" the sheriff said.

"Sure. What's going on?"

When they were out of earshot of the others, in a section of the room that hadn't filled up, the sheriff said to Nels in a hushed voice, "The appointed lawyer for the Bengtson estate has been collecting the mail and trying to organize the bills and statements for the final sale this spring. He brought me this letter addressed to Jake." He pulled the letter from his uniform pocket, opened it, and read it aloud:

> Jake,
>
> I tried reaching you by phone with no luck. I hate to write such belated news, but you need to know that my beloved sister and your wife, Virginia, passed away on December 31, 1993. Her remains were cremated. If you wish to have them and you want to know the details of her death, you can contact me.
>
> The other matter is concerning your son. After Virginia passed, he ran off in the middle of the night. We have no idea where he is. He is more than welcome to stay here in South Dakota, but he doesn't like the rules set by my husband or the work he is supposed to do. I believe that is why Bobby left.
>
> Please contact me and let me know your wishes and if Bobby has shown up in Iowa. I've given you

my address on the envelope. Here is my telephone number: (605) 555-1859.

Betty

"Apparently," said Sheriff Barclay, "the family doesn't know Jake died. Bobby may try to come back home. I trust you'll call me if you see anything unusual at the Bengtson place. I drove out there earlier today but couldn't get up the driveway because it was plowed shut. The lawyer can legally proceed getting the household items and farm equipment ready for the auction now that both Jake and Virginia are dead."

Nels said after a pause, "I might be able to help, Sheriff. I think my grandson Mario knows something."

"Like what?"

"It's something he said about Bobby having no parents and being cold and hungry. Let me talk to him when I get home."

"Nels, if Bobby's around here, we shouldn't wait. What if he is cold and hungry?"

"You're absolutely right, sir. I caught Mario at the Bengtson farm the night before the storm. He said he thought he smelled smoke and decided to go look around the place. He's been acting funny since that time, you know, feeling sorry for Bobby and constantly talking about him. Before Bobby and his mother disappeared, Mario did his best to keep away from Bobby. They didn't get along at all."

"Sounds like I need to take another run out there," said the sheriff. "Do you want to go with me?"

"Sure thing. I'm dressed warm and wearing my snow boots. I came here with Tommy. He's got one of those all-terrain vehicles that can climb mountains. Shall I ask him to drive us?"

"Well, if the kid is out there at the farm, the headlights and noise of the engine might spook him. I think it's best to catch him off guard, maybe walk up from the road. I have a key to the house. We'll stop by headquarters and pick it up, and I'll put on my own heavy boots. We won't need the all-terrain vehicle unless Tommy wants to come with us."

"No, I think he'll want to stay. We have evidence of some shady business taking place at the grain elevator to bring up at the meeting. I'll let him know where we're going," Nels said to the sheriff.

Sheriff Barkley dimmed the squad car headlights as he and Nels approached the farm. The road had been cleared, but a levee of snow was blocking the entrance to the driveway. Parking along the road, the sheriff and Nels climbed over the ice-packed barricade and made their way toward the house.

There was no sign of habitation anywhere—no smoke, no foot tracks, no lights. Climbing the porch stairs, they ceased their conversation. The sheriff turned the key in the lock and listened as the door creaked open. It was the only sound heard in the cold, dark house.

Then he and Nels stepped inside, using flashlights to scan the premises. They found cooled ashes piled up in the potbelly stove. What used to be candles were now nothing but melted wax on tables in each room. Empty peanut butter jars, mason canning jars, brown eggshells, and soup cans littered the kitchen. Among the debris were milk bottles from Swenson Dairy.

"Yep, someone's staying here all right," the sheriff whispered. "I'll go downstairs. You check the upstairs," he said.

In ten minutes, the two men met back in the kitchen. "I looked in every nook and cranny, behind every door, and under beds," said Nels.

"Me too. What about the barn and outbuildings?" said Sheriff Barclay. At that precise moment, the unlatched storm door flapped against the exterior of the house, causing both of them to jump in alarm.

Barclay grabbed for his gun.

Once the shock was over, with the flapping noise continuing,

Nels pulled the inside door open. "There's tracks leading out the door and across the field," he said to Barclay.

"Anyone attached to them?" the sheriff asked.

"No. And they're not fresh. Whoever it is, they're headed in the direction of my place. Kinley's been complaining about the hens' output and spilled milk on the dairy floor. Either Bobby's been helping himself or Mario's been bringing him provisions."

"Let's go and have a talk with that grandson of yours."

Back in the squad car, Nels watched the road for any signs of Bobby. "Take it slow, Sheriff. I'll watch the ditch over on this side. Maybe I can see where the tracks come across the field to the road. Clever little guy to hide his trail."

They were just about to the Swenson farm's driveway when he spotted large gaps in the snowy ditch ahead that led toward his barn across the road. Another tunnel penetrated the snow on the other side of the road. "Hold on there, Sheriff. Can you shine the headlights over there?" Nels said, pointing to the barn. "There's something red lying there in the barnyard."

Sheriff Barkley exclaimed, "Oh Lord God, please don't let it be the boy. I don't know about you, Nels, but I'm not up for climbing the steep icy gully and trying to get over the fence, especially if it turns out to be something blown off someone's clothesline."

"Just pull around into the driveway so we can get to it easier," directed Nels.

CHAPTER 18

Nels knew it would be easier to go through the inside of the barn to reach the heap lying outside in a drift than for either of them to climb through the ditch and go over the fence.

"Well, it's not some lady's bathrobe," he said to Barkley. "It's young Bobby." *I should have been more aware of Mario's behavior. If anything happens to this kid, I'll never forgive myself.*

The red backpack strapped on Bobby's back was stuffed with clothes, some of which were hanging out through the broken zipper. Bobby had wrapped a heavy blanket around the outside of his thin jacket, and his sockless feet were frozen to ragged sneakers.

Nels had tears in his eyes as he brushed snow away from the frozen child. A slight moan came from deep inside the boy when he cradled him against the warmth of his own body.

"Can you get him inside, Nels? I'll call for an ambulance. Look how the poor kid is dressed. Tell your wife not to use warm or hot water on him. He needs to thaw out gradually to prevent frostbite."

"Yes, sir." Nels lifted Bobby, heavy wet blanket and all, as if he were weightless, and ran the hundred yards toward the house. He startled Kinley and the boys when he broke through the back door carrying the icy bundle.

Kinley gasped. "Who is this, Nels?"

Mario began to cry. "It's Bobby. Oh dear Jesus, forgive me. I'm sorry, Grandpa. I'm so sorry," he wailed. "Is he dead?"

"Not yet," Nels replied. "Help me out here, boys." He threw the blanket on the floor. "Mario, get his shoes off and massage his feet. Hans, go get the quilt off your bed."

Icy crystals were stuck to Bobby's eyelashes and to the shaft of hair that had crept out of his knit hat. His face, a grayish color, showed no signs of life.

"Grandpa, are you sure he's not dead?"

"No, he has a slight pulse. The sheriff has an ambulance on the way."

"The sheriff!" Mario said in a shocked voice. "How does he know?"

As Nels stripped off Bobby's wet clothes, he answered, "We'll talk about that later."

Sheriff Barkley walked in as Nels was covering the boy with the quilt Hans had brought from upstairs.

Mario stopped his task of massaging Bobby's feet and stared at Sheriff Barclay, fear written on his face. He began to shake. "Are you here to arrest me?"

"No, son. We're going to work on getting Bobby better and then get him help. But how long have you kept this secret?"

"About a week," Mario stammered.

Kinley raised her voice as she looked at Mario. "You knew about this?"

Mario nodded.

"I hear the ambulance coming," Hans shouted over them.

Nels helped the paramedics carry the gurney to the transport once they had checked Bobby's vital signs. Greeley hospital in Ames was the closest emergency facility. Bobby started to breathe heavily as they loaded him into the ambulance, but he didn't regain consciousness before he left the farm. Sheriff Barkley led the way with the sirens from both vehicles cutting through the freezing air.

If Bobby came here to steal more food, why did he have his backpack filled with clothes? Was he going to ask for help or hoping to stay? By the looks of the inside of his house, it's a wonder he didn't burn the place down. These were Nels's thoughts as he headed back inside the house.

Sheriff Barclay called the Swensons at nine thirty that night. "It looks like the boy will survive. He's coherent now and asking for something to eat. They said he could lose a couple of toes and fingers, but only time will tell. They have forbidden me to question him tonight, so I'm getting ready to leave. Just wanted you to know the outcome. How's your grandson doing, Nels?"

"He's so distraught right now, I didn't feel good about lecturing him."

"Sounds like the right move. Well, good night, and thanks for your help. You saved the kid's life."

First thing the next morning, when the sheriff got to his office, he dialed the number of Mrs. Bengtson's sister in South Dakota.

"This is Sheriff Barclay in Story County, Iowa. Am I speaking with Virginia Bengtson's sister Betty?"

"Yes," the woman answered. "Do you have news about my nephew Bobby?"

"Yes, ma'am. We found Bobby. He had been living alone at the farm. Jake Bengtson died sometime in late summer. We found his decomposed body outside. We were not able to determine how long he had been dead or the cause of death. Did he have any medical condition that you know of, such as heart problems or diabetes?"

"Virginia never talked much about Jake."

"Did she tell you why she left him?"

"There was some kind of disturbance between them. Virginia refused to talk about it, and the convoluted story Bobby told was so wild and crazy that we questioned if it really happened. I never believed half the things that kid said. He lied a lot, and Virginia covered for him. You'll have to ask Bobby to tell you. I can't remember all the details."

"What was the cause of Virginia's death?" *Something serious must have happened. The poor woman died.*

"She died of an infection in her shoulder. It was a wound that wouldn't heal, and she refused to see a doctor. The coroner who did the autopsy said it was caused by a bullet lodged under her armpit."

"Did he save the bullet? If so, I'd like to have it."

"I'm not sure, Sheriff. Will you be sending her kid back to South Dakota?"

Betty was definitely not a good source of information. She had offered little insight into the mystery at the Bengtsons' farm. She was vague, so the sheriff decided that he would be vague too. "Not anytime soon, ma'am. Bobby is recovering from frostbite after living in a deserted house without heat, without electricity, and with little to eat. It seems that even under those circumstances, he'd rather be here than back in South Dakota."

"I guess. I could come to Iowa for a couple of weeks to care for him, but I can't be away any longer than that." She paused, then said, "What will happen to the farm?"

"The farm will be up for auction this spring. As for Bobby, you will not need to come. I'm here if you have further questions."

There was a hesitation before Betty said goodbye. "Uh, I don't know if this is the proper time to mention it, but there are bills we paid to have my sister cremated and other expenses we'd like to get back after the auction and the house is sold."

"I'll bring it to the attention of the estate lawyer, ma'am."

"Thank you for calling, Sheriff. Glad I could help."

When Sheriff Barclay walked into Bobby's hospital room an hour later, the boy was propped up in bed. The first thing the sheriff noticed were the two blackened toes on Bobby's left foot, which were hanging out from beneath the covers. The second thing was the panicked look on Bobby's face as he approached the bed.

"Are you here to arrest me? Where will you send me? juvie hall? back to South Dakota? an orphanage or foster home?" His pained face and distressed voice dissolved into tears as he held up his wrists for the sheriff to cuff. "Dang that rat Mario. I knew I never should've trusted him."

Sheriff Barclay took Bobby's left hand and caressed the ring finger and pinkie, which were the same dark color of the boy's frostbitten toes. "Bobby, I'm here to help you. I'm really sorry to hear about your mother."

"I'll be okay," he said, lying back against the pillow.

"It wasn't Mario who revealed your secret. Your aunt Betty alerted me that you might have come back to Iowa. Mario only talked to me after Mr. Swenson and I found you frozen in the snow outside his barn."

"I don't have a home anymore!" Bobby cried. "My mom was the only one who cared about me. My dad was mean, but Uncle Fred was mean too. He kicked me in the hind end more than once. I figured if I was going to live with mean all the time, I might as well be here with my dad and people I know."

"Why did you and your mother leave Iowa, Bobby?"

"It all started when that little runt Mario and I got into a fight at school and he bested me in front of all our classmates. It made me a laughingstock. We both got suspended for three days. My daddy gave me a good whupping as usual, but when I went back to school, the bruises were still there and Principal Wheaton reported it. Some social worker guy came to the farm asking my dad a lot of questions. He said Dad needed to get counseling if he couldn't find a less violent way to punish me and that social services would do a follow-up check just to make sure it didn't happen again."

Sheriff Barkley felt very sympathetic as he listened. "How did your daddy feel about what the man said?"

"I'd never seen him so mad. After the guy left, I got the shakes and I wanted to run off, but my legs wouldn't move. I ended up getting one of the worst whippings ever. Mama was crying. She thought my dad was going to kill me and begged him to stop. She pulled at his arms and tried to push him away, but he turned and battered her too. That's when I grabbed the rifle, standing by the door, and pointed it at him. I said, 'Get your hands off her or I'll blow your head off.'"

"So, you shot him and buried him in the pigpen?"

"No. No. That's not what happened. I thought he knew I meant business because he did stop and come toward me with a devilish smile, then snatched the gun away."

Sheriff Barkley waited patiently while Bobby made an emotional pause. He handed him the box of Kleenex from his hospital tray. When he thought the boy was ready, he asked, "What happened next, Bobby?"

"He set the gun back by the door and reached for the leather riding crop on the table next to it; that was his usual weapon of punishment. I knew I was in for more.

"He struck me numerous times with the crop until I fell to the floor, and then I felt his boots kicking me as I tried to crawl away.

"Even though Mama was hurt, she didn't give up. I saw her pick up a piece of firewood next to the stove and use it to clobber him something fierce. He teetered and stumbled forward before he lost his balance and fell. We both just stared, waiting for him to make a move, but he didn't; he just rubbed his head.

"'Go get your things. We're leaving,' my mom whispered.

"'I'm not sure I can move. My side hurts,' I said.

"She felt around the pain in my side. She thought I might have had a couple of broken ribs. Then she helped me up, and I leaned on her going up the stairs to pack. We just left my dad sitting on the floor.

"When we came back down, he was gone. We grabbed what we could and loaded it in the truck. I saw him out feeding the pigs. When he realized what we were doing, he came running.

"Mama didn't drive, so she handed me the keys. It took me a little time to get in the truck because of my pain, but I was able to start the truck before my dad reached us.

"He rushed inside the house and came out with the rifle. By then, we were almost to the road, but he fired on us. I heard the bullets hit a couple of times. He was still chasing us after we were on the road. The last bullet I heard came through the back window and hit Mom. I drove as fast as that old heap would go, scared out of my wits."

"So, your dad was alive when you left the farm?"

"Yeah! Last I saw him, he was running after us like a maniac. When he was mad about something, he'd, like, go crazy."

"Are you sure you didn't follow him to the pigpen and shoot him after he beat the two of you?"

"No, sir. It happened just like I said." Picking up from where he had left off, Bobby said, "I was afraid my dad would call you or the police to catch us, so Mom and I kept to the back roads all the way to the border. That's where we ran out of gas and one of the tires went flat. We just left that piece of crap where it died, and we walked to the nearest gas station and called Aunt Betty."

"Your aunt Betty said your mom had an infected wound and the doctor found a bullet in it after she died."

"She never complained, but I saw blood on her dress. At Aunt Betty's, she got sicker and sicker. She wouldn't see a doctor because we didn't have any money or insurance, and she was afraid of an investigation. Plus, she didn't want Dad to find us."

"So, she just kept it to herself?" Sheriff Barclay asked.

"Yeah. We knew about the sore, but I never saw it. It was under her armpit, I guess, close to her heart."

"Oh my. Didn't your aunt and uncle try to help her?"

"No. We were worthless to them if we didn't work. Uncle Fred kept reminding us we were becoming a burden, eating his food, using too much water, always needing something. That's another reason I don't want to go back there."

"Bobby, I think that's enough for today. You do what the nurses and doctors tell you and get well. I'll be back tomorrow. Do you happen to remember the doctor's name who found the bullet?"

"Yeah, Fenway, like the ballpark in Boston."

Sheriff Barclay gave him a big smile and a thumbs-up and left. *This case is getting personal now. I'm going to make sure this kid finds a good home.*

CHAPTER 19

After a night of restlessness following his grandfather's lecture about not reporting Bobby or getting him to safety, Mario came downstairs to the breakfast table. "Can we go see Bobby today?"

Grandpa slipped into his down-filled parka for morning chores. "It might be too soon. We'll wait and give him more time to heal."

"I want him to know I never told on him, even though I know now I should have. I am sorry, Grandpa. I hope you believe me."

"You used poor judgment, but I know you thought you were being a friend to Bobby without realizing the danger you put him in."

"Why do you think his backpack had nothing but clothes in it?"

"I don't know. After the mess Sheriff Barclay and I saw at his house, I'd say he was running out of food and firewood, maybe ready to give up."

"He didn't light the stove during the day," Mario said. "I saw him leave our barn late one afternoon right before Grandma complained about the egg shortage and milk all over the dairy floor. I hope he doesn't lose his toes and fingers because of me."

Mario's grandma came into the kitchen wrapped in her bathrobe and with curlers in her hair. "The kid had his nerve all right, but please don't start placing blame on yourself, Mario. It will all work out. Right now, go find Hans and get started on your chores. I'll have breakfast ready when you're done."

"Did I hear breakfast?" Hans said, wandering into the room in a sleepy stupor.

"Chores first," Grandma said.

"You mean I left my warm bed only to be thrown outside in the freezing cold? We'll probably end up like Bobby. What kind of mom does that to her kids? What are you fixing anyway?" he whined.

"Pancakes and sausage."

He rushed to put on his coat. "Okay, I'm on it. I love pancakes. I'd do anything for pancakes. Make me a dozen."

Mario added, "We haven't had pancakes for weeks."

"That's because we haven't had extra eggs to use up, thanks to Bobby. I'm still a little short on eggs, but pancakes it is this morning."

After chores, the family gathered around the table. Tommy arrived to join them.

"How'd the meeting go after I left? Did you get to present our concerns about the grain elevator?" Grandpa asked.

"Yes I did, and it seems that other farmers who employ migrant workers have experienced similar problems," Tommy answered.

Grandpa shook his head. "Were any of the co-op board members there?"

"There were at least two of them. They claimed to have no knowledge that anything was amiss. Cooper said it was the first he'd heard of it."

Grandpa prodded further. "What about the supervisor. Did he show up?"

"Yeah, he was there. He claimed innocence even though Johnson and I said we had spoken to him personally about shorting us per bushel and taking the white farmers and field hands ahead of our Mexican employees," said Tommy. "Cooper and the other board members acted like they were not happy about the situation and promised to look into it further. The supervisor walked out before the meeting was adjourned."

"Well, if we don't notice any change or action before the next couple of meetings, we should make a motion to have the guy fired," Grandpa said.

"I agree," said Tommy. "After hanging around after the meeting, I got home late last night. Peg said they found the Bengtson kid here in the snow."

Devouring his fifth pancake, Hans spoke up, saying, "He was frozen to the ground like a side of beef out by the barn."

"Hans, don't be so flippant and crass," Grandma scolded.

"It's true," Hans continued. "Mario had to massage his feet. He might lose some toes and fingers."

"Wow!" Tommy reacted. "What happens to him now?"

All eyes around the table looked at Grandpa, everyone waiting for his answer.

"That seems to be the question everyone is asking," Grandpa replied. "Since he only has a few minor infractions against him, such as running away and skipping school, I don't believe he deserves juvie time for that. The kid's lived a hard life and had his reasons."

"That leaves foster care or putting him up for adoption," Tommy concluded.

"Nobody in their right mind would adopt him," Hans mused.

Grandma reprimanded him again. "Hans, please try to show some compassion. But for the grace of God, that could have been you."

Mario listened to the conversation but kept silent. *Bobby is me. I have no mother or father. I had no happy home at one time. The only difference is I had family who loved me and took me in. Bobby doesn't have anyone to come to his rescue.*

Grandma began clearing dishes from the table.

Grandpa finally broke the silence that had left everyone thinking. "We'll have to wait and see how things turn out. But I've been considering taking Bobby in."

The dishes Grandma was carrying crashed to the floor. "Nels, no!"

"Just let me finish," he said. "We could be his foster parents until things are settled. Sort of a trial period. If he doesn't work out here, we haven't permanently committed to anything."

"I can't believe you, Nels. It would be nothing but continual chaos."

Hans wailed, "Dad, please say you're kidding! Don't do this to us. Right, Mom? Right, Mario?"

Mario smiled. "I think it's a great idea."

Tommy rapped his knuckles on the table and held up his hands to quiet everyone. "I remember another messed-up kid who came here to live. He had a lot to learn about life. After a summer of loving discipline from this man"—he gestured toward Grandpa— "my life changed. I went back to school, graduated from Iowa State, and became a husband and father."

Grandma had tears in her eyes. "How could I forget?" She came over, hugged Tommy, and planted a kiss on his cheek, then moved around the table and did the same to Grandpa.

Grandpa responded by kissing her back. "What do you think, hon? Can we give Bobby a try?"

"Yes. I'll do my part. Boys, we'll expect you to welcome him too." She looked at each Hans and Mario as she spoke.

"Aw, Mom, I voted no," said Hans.

"It's a great idea, Grandma. Thank you."

Tommy put both his thumbs up. "That makes enough of us to keep the lad busy and out of trouble."

I never thought the day would come that I'd care what happened to Bobby after all the mean things he did to me. Maybe this will make up for me not doing the right thing when I discovered he was back.

CHAPTER 20

Bobby listened as the social worker spoke. "Bobby, I'm sad to say that most couples on the adoption roster are looking for a newborn or a child under four. Even with your sweetest smile, it won't be enough to convince prospective parents you'd make a nice addition to their family. We normally try to place children with relatives or in foster homes, but at present, all our foster homes in the area are overflowing. Are there any family members who would be willing to take you in?"

"I would rather stand before a firing squad than go back to live with Aunt Betty and Uncle Fred in South Dakota. They only want to use me as a field hand, and they're stingy."

Bobby had told Sheriff Barclay and the estate lawyer the same thing, and the court's decision had ruled out his aunt and uncle as his legal guardians.

When Mr. Swenson offered to let him stay temporarily at Swenson Farms, while social services continued to search for a permanent residence, Bobby was elated.

Mrs. Swenson made him a comfortable bed in what used to be Mr. Swenson's office, which was moved upstairs into a nursery-size room next to Mario's room.

"This is going to work out fine because Mario is doing most of the bookkeeping now on the computer," she said to Bobby.

"I don't even know what that is," he replied.

"And when I fall asleep at my desk," Mr. Swenson said, laughing, "she can wheel me across the hall and put me in bed."

Mr. Swenson was such a jolly, kind fellow. It was the reason Bobby had come to the Swensons' farm the night they found him in the snow. He had run out of options, but most of all he longed for some kind of human contact. In his dreams, he drooled over hot delicious home-cooked meals with all the fixings, and he knew Mrs. Swenson was the kind of woman who served her family those types of dinners.

Bobby planned to use his best manners but knew he had more rough edges than were allowed at the Swensons', especially his language and attitude.

Mr. Nels (the name that seemed to stick to his new parent figure) was patient in correcting him.

Once after a vulgarity slipped out, Mr. Nels took him aside, away from the others. "Now, son, that's not how we talk around here. An oopsie now and then is permissible, but in two weeks' time, I expect that to improve or else you will start to suffer consequences. My boys aren't allowed to swear, bully others, or hurt others with name-calling or mean behavior, and you will be expected to behave in the same way. Do we understand each other?"

"Yes, Mr. Nels. I'll try harder."

Mr. Nels gave him a side hug that turned into a pat on the back. "That's all I ask, son."

Son. He called me son. Is it possible I can fit in here?

Hans kept his distance but never missed an opportunity to challenge Bobby under his breath through gritted teeth. "If you make one more snide remark about my weight, it will be worth it to me to clean your plow and take my punishment," he had said one day.

Bobby found common ground with Mario, however, even though they were two totally different personalities. They played chess and other competitive board games a lot, and best of all, Mario taught him how to box.

Bobby was amazed at the setup in the barn the first time Mario took him out to practice. He hadn't seen this part when he was sneaking in and pilfering milk from the dairy. Each section seemed to have its own space, unlike the small barn at the pig farm, where everything stayed where it landed when thrown inside.

"You're having problems with balancing your feet, Bobby. You need to put more weight on the back foot," said Mario.

"Even with these new sneakers Mr. Nels bought me, it still hurts to use my full weight on the left foot. It's only been a month since they removed the top joints on those two toes. I may never have good balance on that foot."

"If it doesn't get stronger with time, you'll just start to develop your own style then," Mario encouraged. "I think we'd better get back to the house. I promised Grandma we'd do our homework before bedtime."

"Can't we play Monopoly instead? I hate to study. How do you live with so many rules?"

"It's how Grandma and Grandpa raised me. I know you're behind on your schoolwork because you were gone a whole semester. I can help you when I'm finished with mine," Mario offered.

"Nah. Your grandma explains things better. She is very patient with me."

Kinley received her first summons, on Bobby's behalf, to meet with Ms. Reed, the English teacher, six weeks after she had enrolled him.

"Mrs. Swenson, I will probably be stating the obvious when I say this, but Bobby has fallen so far behind that I think it best if he is held back from entering junior high for another year. I'm not sure it's a decision you want to make as his temporary guardian, but that is my recommendation. I do see an improvement in his attitude and willingness to try harder since he's come back, but I don't believe it's enough to move him on to seventh grade."

"Oh, Ms. Reed, how horribly devastating for Bobby. I don't know what it was like for him in class before, but he has really tried hard to keep up and almost seems to enjoy it. I think it might bring him down again if he doesn't move on with his classmates."

"I know, Mrs. Swenson. I'm feeling the same way. But the big picture is to get him properly educated. Most of his problems revolve around reading and comprehending, which carries over into his other classes too. I've discussed it with his other teachers and have found he is struggling in their classes also. Would you rather not make the decision?"

Kinley spoke up boldly: "Ms. Reed, if you can give me a list of areas where he needs improvement, I will devote a lot of time this summer to working with him. I'll start by enrolling him in summer school, giving him extra tutoring and fewer chores on the farm, so by the time school starts in the fall, if there is no improvement, maybe we can have this discussion again. That's my decision."

"So, you want us to pass him on and hope he makes enough progress over the summer to start grade seven?"

"Yes," said Kinley.

"I'll tell his other teachers and Principal Wheaton what's been decided. You and your family have really been good for Bobby. I hope it continues."

"Thank you, Ms. Reed." Kinley left with a feeling of unease. She hoped she was up for the challenge that had just been presented to her. *All I can do is try. I'll leave the rest up to Bobby and the Lord.*

Winter dragged on. It was the last week of April before the weather changed to warmer temperatures and the danger of frost had passed. May was full of showers and flooding along the Skunk River, which bordered the Swenson farm. Once the mud and mire in the fields dried up, planting could get under way.

Bobby had been there since the end of January. Although their living conditions were more than acceptable, the boys were anxious to get outside and saddle up the horses when the spring air called.

"You've ridden before, haven't you, Bobby?"

"Just old Barney our mule," he said. "He was shorter and slower, but we got along fine. We had no need for horses on a pig farm."

Mario helped him up on Windy's back behind him. "You can ride with me for now, but when Lupita comes for the summer, she always rides with me."

"Well, he's not riding with me," said Hans, spurring Buck into action.

"With your fat butt, there's probably no room left in the saddle anyway," Bobby shouted as Hans departed. Then he said to Mario, "Can we ride over to the pig farm? I left a mess there. I should take out the trash and go through some of the things I don't want put in the auction. I can't think of what that would be, but maybe one last look just in case."

Mario reined Windy in the direction of the pig farm. "Don't you have a favorite toy or memento from when you were a little kid? You should keep at least some pictures of your parents and some of yourself when you were a baby."

"Nah, they don't mean nothing to me," said Bobby.

"What about some of your dad's tools, or the books your mom used to read to you?"

"Yeah, I'll look for the strap my dad used to beat me with. I should keep it as a reminder of how much I hated him, or save it to use on my own kids someday. I tore up the *Snipp, Snapp, and Snurr* book Mom used to read to me. I hated the kids in that book. Maybe we shouldn't go there after all."

"Don't say those things, Bobby. I'm sorry for all the pain you suffered, but that's all over now. You can start a new life. I lost my mom when I was five, and I never got to know my dad much until a few years before he died. He hurt me in a different way with broken promises and many missed visits. I forgave him and also forgave myself for thinking I had done something wrong that made him stay away."

"I suppose you're right. But that stuff is all new to me," Bobby said reluctantly.

There was a car parked by the house and the front door was open when they reached the pig farm.

Mario dismounted. "Come on."

"Nah. We'd better not. I don't want to get into any more trouble."

"I'm going in with or without you. What's the worst that could happen?"

Bobby stayed seated on Windy, insisting there was nothing of importance he wanted in the house. "This was a mistake to come here. Forget it. I want to go back."

"Nope. I'm going in," Mario said, climbing the front steps.

"Okay," Bobby said, following Mario.

Two women were inside organizing boxes and labeling them. "Hello there," one of them said. "Can we help you with something?"

Mario stepped in as Bobby hung back in the doorway. "This is my friend Bobby Bengtson's farm. He would like to look around if that's okay. He wants to make sure he didn't leave anything behind."

The other woman said, "Sure. Come on in. There are two boxes of family photos, documents, and personal items over there on the table." She pointed. "They will be taken to the estate lawyer's office if you don't take them."

"Bobby?" Mario looked in Bobby's direction and motioned for him to enter.

"Yeah. Maybe if you taped them shut, it wouldn't be a problem," Bobby said.

"Do you want to go through them first?" the woman asked.

Bobby replied, "Nah."

Mario could tell the question had made his friend uncomfortable. He wasn't ready to take a trip down memory lane, and he'd probably feel better once the cartons were sealed.

"If there's anything else, now's the time to take it," the woman said as she finished taping.

Bobby went over to the leather whip by the door. He picked it up and laid it on top of the cardboard boxes. "Let's go," he said to Mario, gathering up the boxes.

"I don't know why you would want that riding crop, Bobby."

"It's my business. I'm taking it," he said.

Once the boys were astride Windy, the woman handed Bobby the boxes. Mario and Bobby made it to the road before one carton fell off.

Bobby jumped down from Windy to retrieve it. A truck came up from behind and stopped on the road beside them.

"You need some help?" Henry Morales asked, grinning.

Mario climbed off Windy to greet him. "Senor Henry, what a welcome surprise. Are you coming to help with the crops again?"

"Sí, Mario, but I am alone. Carmen and Lupita are busy with the baby." He opened his wallet to display a picture of the newest addition to their family. "His name is Enrique, like me—Henry in English."

"Look, Bobby." Mario held the picture out in front of him.

"Just another taco belly," Bobby said with disgust.

"Watch what you say, Bobby. If you say anything like that again, I will tell Grandpa."

Bobby scowled at Mario.

"Seriously, Bobby. Senor Henry is like family to us. We have nothing but respect for him. This is one thing Grandpa will not give you a second chance to get right."

Senor opened the passenger door. "Throw those boxes in the truck."

"No. They're my boxes, and I don't want you to touch them," Bobby said.

"Well then, you can carry them home. And expect Grandpa to be waiting for you," Mario snapped. Then he turned away, mounted Windy, and rode off, leaving Bobby standing by the cartons.

Henry Morales laughed and sat silently for a few moments, then said, "Put your boxes in the back of the truck and get in, young man."

Bobby picked up the boxes, threw them in the truck bed, then hopped in beside them, his feet dangling over the tailgate.

Henry smiled and waved at Mario as they passed. *¡Caramba! It's going to be a long season.*

CHAPTER 21

One day in late April, Kinley was sitting at the kitchen table with Bobby, listening as Mario and Hans began planning their thirteenth birthdays in the family room. Since Mario had come to live at the farm, the boys, only six weeks apart, had always celebrated their birthdays together somewhere in between their birthdates.

She covered her ears to drown out the noise as they argued over going to the Roller Cade or spending the day at the Science Center in Des Moines.

"When is your birthday, Bobby?"

"I was thirteen last October," he answered.

Kinley thought for a moment. *He must have been held back in school at one point or started school a year late.* She felt glad she'd made the decision not to hold him back another year. It made her even more determined to help him get caught up.

When school was finally out for the summer, the daily schedule changed at the farm. Hans worked the fields with his father, Henry, and Tommy, planting, fertilizing, and fence mending. Mario stayed home to help Kinley with the dairy business and the garden, to log sales and expenses into the computer for Nels, and to perform other household duties, giving Kinley more time to bring Bobby up to standards.

Kinley's routine for Bobby included driving him to summer school three days a week, taking him to visit the library whenever he ran out of books, and letting him select books that were easy to read (below sixth grade level). As he became proficient and comfortable with that reading level, she moved him up a degree, which made him struggle harder.

Although Bobby grumbled, sighed, and begged to go with the men, Kinley could see the pride as he conquered each new step of achievement.

One day in midsummer, she said to him, "I think you're going to make it, Bobby. I never told you this, but Ms. Reed wanted to hold you back another grade. You had missed too many classes. Did you even go to school when you were in South Dakota?"

"Nah. Uncle Fred worked me like a pack mule. He said since no one knew I was living there, he wouldn't make me go to school. At first, I thought it was cool, but when I found out what he had in mind, I wished I were in school—anything to get away from him. After my mom died, I wasn't going to stick around."

"Do you like to study now?"

"It's okay, but I'd feel better if I were helping out on the farm."

"What a nice thing to say," Kinley replied. "Can you drive a tractor?"

"Sure! I'm not stupid."

"I think you've studied hard enough today. Why don't you surprise Nels and mow the yard and the ditches with the lawn tractor? The guys are so tired when they get home at night."

"Really? Yes," he said, pumping his arm up and down.

A pattern was established. Bobby's reward for working hard at his studies was a chance to hang out with the menfolk and contribute to the running of the farm. He was a hard worker, both physically and academically, when there was something in it for him. The kid was thriving by the end of summer.

One morning in July, Bobby and Mr. Nels were in the dairy barn attaching milking machines to the dairy cows.

"This sure does beat slopping hogs, trudging through muck and mire, and breathing stinky air," Bobby said to Mr. Nels.

"There can be a good profit in raising pigs, Bobby."

"Guess my dad didn't know that or how to do it right."

"It might have helped if he had had outside help like Henry."

"Oh no, my dad would never hire no foreigner. You can't trust them. They're here taking jobs from Americans."

"Henry is an American, Bobby. His parents came here when he was just a little boy. He even served in the National Guard during the Vietnam War. He's as American as they come. I know there's still people like your dad who have no respect for anyone different from them."

Bobby didn't reply. This was one area he had not made an attempt to improve in. He tolerated Senor Henry when Mr. Nels, Miss Kinley, and the boys were nearby, but he wasn't about to abandon his old habits and predispositions toward this subject.

Just from observation, he had learned how much the Swensons relied on Senor Henry's opinions and ideas, asking for his advice on many issues. Even Tommy, who had a degree in agriculture from Iowa State University, heeded Henry's advice on certain matters. They called it common sense, simple ways, and folk wisdom.

Bobby himself had witnessed Senor Henry (the name the Swensons insisted the boys call him) dress a deer, butcher a pig, and fill a freezer with a side of beef. These were skills only learned from an experienced master, not in a classroom, Mario told him.

It was also common knowledge that Senor Henry's goal in life was to own his own farm one day, but because of his kind heart and generous soul, he helped keep other family members down south out of poverty, thus putting his own future on hold.

Bobby called Senor Henry names in private and spit at him, but not on him, if he disagreed with Senor's orders. But the man never reported him to Mr. Nels or retaliated for his rudeness. He'd just walk away with a smile, avoiding any conflict.

So, Bobby had come to the conclusion that Mr. Nels deliberately had partnered him to work with Senor Henry, hoping the friction between them would ease over time as they got to know each other. *It won't work, Mr. Nels.*

Bobby was picked up from his last day of summer school by Miss Kinley and Mario. They headed to the library in Ames to return books and check out new ones, then arrived home just seconds before Senor Henry drove in behind them.

He motioned for all of them to come over to where he had parked.

Mario ran toward Senor Henry's old truck, but Bobby lagged behind with Miss Kinley, knowing he'd be spending the rest of the afternoon with Senor.

"What's this?" Mario asked, peering in the truck bed.

"What do you think, Bobby?" Senor Henry gestured as he came to look inside.

Lying on a pile of blankets was the most beautiful black colt. Its shiny coat glistened in the sun, its dark eyes showing a fear of its audience. It whinnied, trying to get up. It was perfect in every way except for one leg tucked beneath its body. It struggled to get up several times in the tight quarters of the truck bed before it gave up and fell back on the blankets.

"What do you plan to do with it, Senor?" Mario asked.

"I'm not sure. Neighbor Johnson said he planned to shoot it unless someone took it off his hands. I couldn't bear the thought. Look how beautiful it is. I believe its mother has a string of championship ribbons. This young colt just doesn't fit in with Johnson's thoroughbreds."

"How old is it?" Bobby finally commented after looking it over.

"Johnson said nine, almost ten months. It's weaned and gelded. It's not 100 percent perfect, but what a beauty," he repeated. "I was hoping Nels would let me find a place in the barn to keep the colt and let me work with him." As an afterthought, he added, "I don't think Johnson would really have shot it. He just didn't want it."

"Oh, there's plenty of room in the barn, Henry. You have my permission," said Miss Kinley.

"Thanks, Grandma," Mario said.

"What do you think, Bobby?" Senor Henry asked again.

"Just a good-for-nothing lame horse," Bobby replied, but his heart was touched by the damaged yearling—helpless, unloved by its rightful owner, and with no hope for a successful future. Yes, Bobby could relate to its misfortune.

"Let's go find a stall for it," said Kinley, leading the way to the barn with Henry and Mario following.

Bobby stayed with the colt. He jumped in the truck bed with the dark horse. He stroked its ebony coat and stringy mane and tail. His hand ended up caressing the crippled limb, feeling the misshapen bone structure with the tips of his fingers. The colt nuzzled his arm and rested its head on his thigh.

Bobby jumped out of the truck when he saw the others returning.

"Okay, you two, I'll drive down closer to the barn, and I'll need your help getting him out and settled in the stall," said Senor Henry.

Mario got in front with Senor, and Bobby climbed back in with the colt. The transition took place easily. The fear in the colt's eyes had all but disappeared.

"Kinley," said Henry, massaging the colt's malformed leg, "I'd like to have the vet come take a look at it. It may need a few bones broken and reset. I can't do that, but I can take it from there. I'll pay for it."

"You'll do no such thing, Henry. I'll give the vet a call."

"This will be my personal project. I can't expect you to do that."

"You didn't ask. I volunteered," she answered.

Bobby hadn't left the horse's side. "Do you really think his leg can be fixed, Senor Henry?" It was the first time he had addressed Senor Henry properly.

"We'll see, Bobby."

CHAPTER 22

Bobby cringed as he watched the vet break the bone in the colt's damaged leg and stretch the tendons into place.

Wrapping the leg tightly, the vet said to Senor, Bobby, and Mario, "Keep him off of the leg for a week or so. He'll let you know when he's ready to get up. If he keeps trying, help him stand and see what happens. He'll hobble for a while until the leg becomes stronger. He will never be a racehorse or workhorse, but he's a wonderful animal. Keep the leg taped when you exercise him for at least eight to ten weeks. He's going to be fine."

Bobby appointed himself the chief caretaker of the horse, which he called Ebony. He got permission from the Swensons to camp out in the barn all night for a week. He wanted to make sure Ebony didn't try to get up and cause further damage. He talked to the colt and massaged his upper leg, giving him comfort. School would start soon, but for now, he had time to spend with the helpless colt.

"Who gave you the right to name him Ebony?" Hans scowled.

"Yeah, Bobby. Maybe Senor wants him to have a Spanish name," Mario scolded.

"You can call him whatever you like. I'm calling him Ebony," said Bobby, defending himself.

Senor Henry walked in on the discussion. "Ebony fits him just fine. That's what we'll call him. Ebony. I like it."

Bobby smiled. "Thank you."

"Has Ebony tried to stand yet? It's been a week," Senor Henry asked. "If not, I think it's time to get him up and walking."

"Shall we lift him up, Senor?" Hans said.

"It'd be best if he did it on his own, but I think we've created a spoiled horse." Senor laughed as he slipped a rope around Ebony's neck. "Maybe a few tugs will give him the idea."

All three boys tried to coax Ebony up with treats held out at a distance to make him struggle to reach them.

Bobby and Hans finally lifted Ebony's rump as Senor pulled. The colt did the rest with his front legs.

With his body upright and his legs sturdy, the colt ran out the open barn door, dragging the rope, which had slipped from Senor's hand. All four chased after him.

The playful colt seemed to be enjoying the game. Bobby's heart was bursting with love and excitement for this magnificent creature. Ebony, kicking up his back legs, which before had hobbled him, began to wobble, trying to keep balance. Bobby's laughter couldn't be contained.

Victoriously waving his hat, Senor Henry shouted, "Yippee!"

"Your instincts were right, Senor. Look how he runs!" Bobby yelled.

"Now we must catch him before he hurts himself. Bobby! Hans! Git in front and try to grab the rope. But be careful."

Ebony finally slowed down and slightly limped toward Bobby.

Bobby hugged the colt's neck. "You silly boy. You were supposed to take it easy your first time up. Do you think he overdid it, Senor?"

"I think he will be okay. We will keep a close eye on him."

From that day forward, Bobby enthusiastically gave Senor Henry daily updates on Ebony's progress.

After a busy summer, school was back in session. Bobby went to say goodbye to Ebony before joining Hans and Mario as they waited for the school bus.

"Hurry, Bobby, the bus is coming," yelled Mario.

He made it just in time, before the bus doors shut.

"What's it like being in love with a horse, Bobby?" said a boy across the aisle from where Bobby had sat down.

This is Hans's doing, Bobby thought, giving Hans an evil look and trying to ignore the boy who asked the question.

Hans was laughing. "Well, answer Timothy, Bobby. Did you kiss it and give it a big hug?"

"Shut up, moron," Bobby replied, continuing to ignore Timothy.

It was then the bus driver issued a proclamation: "Okay, boys, let's get one thing straight. I'm not putting up with your shenanigans and fights this year. I will not hesitate to put you off the bus regardless of the weather, and you will walk for the next week. Consider yourselves warned."

"You can't do that," said Hans.

"There's one way to find out," said the driver as he shifted into gear. Silence reigned the rest of the way to school.

Two weeks into the new semester, Bobby's teachers were full of praise and admiration for the progress he had achieved in just one summer. At home, he handed Miss Kinley a note from the teacher before going to the barn to see Ebony.

"What's this?" she asked, unfolding the letter.

"I don't know. I usually throw them away, but I couldn't remember doing anything wrong today, so I saved it for you."

"Did you read it?"

"Nah."

She read aloud while he poured a glass of milk:

> Dear Mrs. Swenson,
>
> I want to commend you for the wonderful job you did of helping Bobby catch up with his peers. In speaking with Mr. Wheaton and Bobby's other new teachers, I have concluded that it was a wise choice

not to hold Bobby back a grade. We are very proud of his work and the change in his attitude toward his studies and the other students. Thank you for this.

Sincerely, Ms. Reed

"What good news, Bobby. Your teachers are very proud of your work. Wait till Nels sees this."

"Thanks, Miss Kinley." Bobby tried not to blush but felt his face heating up. He couldn't remember having gotten many compliments, if any, over the years.

"The Department of Human Services will also be pleased to see this report," Kinley added.

His heart sank at her last comment. It was a harsh reminder that he was still in a program to be adopted. What were his chances of ever finding a family like the Swensons? Even Senor Henry was beginning to feel like family.

Depression overcame Bobby as he entered the barn. Would he end up in a home close enough to visit Ebony once in a while? His eyes welled up with tears. The horse nuzzled close to his neck, and he clung to it with a passion he'd never experienced before.

Ebony seemed to understand, neighing softly as Bobby cried.

CHAPTER 23

It was Thursday, the twelfth of October, and school had gotten out early because of the big homecoming game with rival team Ankeny Academy. In terms of the number of junior high and high school students, the schools were comparable in size.

Bobby and Mario took the bus home, but they would return for the game later in the evening. Hans had stayed at school to work with the team, which amounted basically to serving as water boy and equipment gofer.

"What do you want to do?" Mario asked Bobby. "We've got the whole afternoon."

"I don't know. I haven't been back to my home since the auction. The place is probably overgrown with weeds by now, unless someone bought it."

"Okay, let's go." Mario grabbed Windy's saddle from the hooks outside her stall and threw it on her back, fastening it into place.

As they rode, Mario asked, "Know what tomorrow is?"

"Yeah, Friday the thirteenth," Bobby answered.

"It's your birthday, silly."

"Yep. Lucky me, I get to celebrate it on Friday the thirteenth."

"I don't believe in all that superstitious stuff."

"Why do you think they changed the date of our game with Ankeny Academy to tonight instead of playing on Friday?" asked Bobby.

"So, we're going to win because they changed the date?" Mario said mockingly. "Why doesn't that work for the other team too?"

"Well, at least we'll have a better chance. I'm just glad I'm not turning thirteen on Friday the thirteenth. That would be a double whammy."

"What do you mean? How old are you?"

"I'll be fourteen tomorrow."

"What? How come I didn't know that? Do Grandma and Grandpa know?"

"Yep."

Mario prodded Windy into a gallop as they approached what used to be the Bengtsons' farm.

Bobby was astonished as they rode up to the house. "Wow, someone must have bought the place." The house and grounds had changed. The grass had been mown, the trees and bushes had been trimmed, and some repair had begun on the exterior of the house and deteriorating outbuildings.

There were no feelings of sadness as Bobby dismounted Windy and walked around the grounds. In fact, he felt proud as he expressed to Mario, "It's going to make someone a nice little farm. I never pictured it being worth much before. I wonder if Mr. Nels knows who bought it."

"If he doesn't, he knows how to find out; he knows everyone in town. Look, Bobby, you can't even see where the pigs were kept. It's all been leveled off."

Bobby mused as he viewed the spot once occupied by the pigsties. "I wonder if they ever figured out what killed my dad?"

"Will you get any money from the farm?" Mario asked.

"Probably not. I think my dad owed too many bills."

"That's two more questions you need to have Grandpa check into," said Mario.

In their exploration, the boys went down into the root cellar behind the house where Bobby's mother had kept potatoes, turnips, squash, and preserved fruits and vegetables year-round. It was empty except for cobwebs and moldy dampness.

Climbing to the top of the cellar, Mario pointed out the edge of Tommy's property bordering the far north end of Bengtson farm.

"Before Mr. Nels took me in," Bobby said, "I never knew that was part of Swenson Farms, because Tommy's last name is different."

"Tommy is Grandma's son from her first marriage. My mother was Tommy's sister. Hans was a surprise baby after Grandma married Nels."

"I knew the fields across the road from us clear up to the Johnsons' farm belonged to the Swensons though," Bobby said. "I think my dad used to steal corn for the pigs sometimes."

"I'm sure Grandpa knew and didn't care," said Mario, running down the cave hill. "Let's go. We don't want to miss seeing our team win tonight."

"You want to make a bet?" Bobby asked, accepting Mario's extended hand as an aid to get him up on Windy's back.

"Nah. You don't have anything I want."

"You're right."

In the past, Bobby had not gone to many school activities and never a sports event. So, he relished being part of the discussion at school the next day. The excitement of winning the game by one point in the last quarter was relived as the event was discussed in depth for at least half of each class period.

The boys were still chattering about the game as the bus dropped them off at the farm after school. In their excitement, they had failed to notice the decorated dining area off the kitchen, until a balloon floated through the door between the two rooms.

"What's this?" Hans asked. "How long are we going to celebrate the big win?"

"It's Bobby's birthday," said Mario.

Miss Kinley humorously wiped her brow and feigned tiredness. "Yes, I've slaved away all day getting his party ready."

"What?!" said Bobby, charging into the dining room. "Wow! This is for me?" Balloons clung to the ceiling. Gifts were stacked on the buffet next to a birthday cake with chocolate frosting. "Thank you, Miss Kinley. I've never had a party before."

"There'll just be six of us, but it will be a celebration," she said.

"Sorry, Bobby, I didn't get you anything because I didn't know," said Hans.

"Well then, you can contribute by helping me get supper ready," said Miss Kinley.

"What are we having?" asked Hans.

"I've made Bobby's favorite: beef burgers, french fries, sweet corn on the cob, and homemade cake and ice cream. I told Nels and Henry to be back early today."

Around six o'clock, when supper was over, there wasn't a morsel left on the table as Miss Kinley cleared the dishes away and wiped down the table. Mr. Nels set the stack of gifts in front of Bobby and added another box, wrapped in brown paper and tied with twine.

Bobby was quivering inside with excitement, trying to contain his emotions. He wanted to rip into the presents, but he waited politely for Senor Henry to return to the table; he had disappeared momentarily outside.

Bobby's fingers fidgeted with the string on Nels's present until he heard Senor's boots on the porch and the screen door squeak open. Senor Henry's rump was barely in his chair at the table when the brown wrapping fell to the floor. Bobby stared at the bundle of papers inside the box—legal-looking papers.

"What's this?" he said with disappointment, not sure of what he had expected the light weight box to hold.

Mario shot out of his chair and looked over Bobby's shoulder. Then he grabbed the documents out of the box and glanced over them quickly. His mouth gaped open, his eyes widened, and he seemed speechless and in shock.

"What going on?" Bobby asked, unsure why Miss Kinley, Mr. Nels, and Senor Henry were smiling.

Mario pointed out to him a phrase written in fancy letters: "Legal adoption of Robert Bengtson."

Bobby's heart sank as tears filled his eyes. His hands shook as he buried his face in them, crying unashamedly in front of everyone.

"Well, this is not the reaction I expected," said Mr. Nels. "Why are you so sad, Bobby?"

"I knew this day would come. Who adopted me?" he managed to choke out.

Mr. Nels moved over and put his strong arms around Bobby, drawing him against his broad chest.

"Kinley and I thought you'd like to be our son," Nels said in a gentle voice. "Doesn't that make you happy?"

Bobby looked at the document again through blurry eyes and sobbed louder. He felt numb as he shook his head in the affirmative.

The party guests gathered around him for a group hug. Even Hans and Senor Henry wiped at their eyes. "Sorry to be such a baby. It's more than I ever hoped for. Thank you, Mr. Nels and Miss Kinley."

Mr. Nels took Bobby's face in both his hands and drew it close to him. "You're welcome, Son. And from now on, make that Mom and Dad. Okay?"

More tears fell as Bobby answered, "Yes, sir—uh, I mean Dad."

Once Bobby had calmed down, his new mom reminded him of his other presents waiting to be opened. Nothing in the presents set before him could compare with the sense of belonging he felt at that moment; a family was all he wanted, all he needed.

Stacks of nice clothes, shoes, and games rested amid crumpled birthday paper and ribbon. Mario gave Bobby coupons for boxing lessons, and Hans, after rummaging through his room, handed Bobby his collection of *Star Wars* cards.

Senor Henry interrupted Bobby as he was thanking everyone for their gifts. "Hold on there, boy, you're not done yet." He left the table and came back seconds later, carrying a worn-out saddle.

"That's the saddle I used on our old mule Barney. Poor Barney, he was the closest I ever came to having my own horse. Where'd you get his saddle, Senor?" Bobby's fingers caressed the faded leather finish and touched the notches along one edge of the saddle that he had made each time his father had beaten Barney for his stubbornness. The last notch was the one Barney didn't survive.

"I bought it at your farm auction for a few pennies. It's still got some life left in it. I thought you might need it for your horse when he's ready to ride."

"Say what?" Bobby exclaimed.

"I'll be heading back to Texas soon after harvest. I can't take Ebony with me, and I couldn't think of a better caretaker." Senor smiled.

"I'll be glad to care for him while you're gone, Senor Henry."

"Bobby, Ebony is yours now. Is that so hard to accept?"

"Oh, Senor Henry, seriously?" he exclaimed. "I'm all cried out. I didn't think it could get any better. Oh God, this is too much." More tears did indeed come.

Where did all these tears come from? Is it that I stored them up, waiting for the right moment for them to spill out? I cried many times over whippings, but these tears are different; they're tears from a joyful, grateful heart.

Having witnessed the Swensons hugging each other all the time for no particular reason, Bobby shyly reached out and put his arms around Senor's neck. It actually felt good as Senor Henry patted his back in the manly embrace. *Senor must be coming down with something. That's the second time he's wiped his eyes.*

After the dining room had cleared of adults, Bobby said to Mario and Hans, "Maybe Friday the thirteenth is my lucky day."

CHAPTER 24

It was the time of year when the weather takes a turn and changes from fall to winter overnight before all the crops make it to market or into storage bins. A cold front in November had changed the smiling faces of the Swensons' Halloween jack-o'-lanterns on the front porch into grotesque smirks of wrinkled old men.

It was Veteran's Day, and the south acres of Swenson Farms across from the Bengtson place still had corn to harvest.

Henry Morales hoisted the American flag up the flagpole, as he did every morning, and saluted it before following Nels to the south fields. Boss Nels had kept the boys home from school to help.

Hans rode in the John Deere corn picker with Tommy, and Mario and Nels pulled a wagon alongside the picker, accepting the cleaned corn it shelled out.

Bobby and Henry pulled a second wagon alongside neighbor Johnson, who was using his picker to help since his crops were already in for the season. By two thirty in the afternoon, Henry and Bobby pulled away with the last load of corn and headed for town.

Henry found a lengthy line at the co-op and turned the corner behind the lineup to keep from blocking traffic at the intersecting street. "I think the weather caught everyone off guard," he said to Bobby.

"I've never been to the grain elevators before. We took our pigs to livestock auctions or the packinghouse for slaughter," said Bobby.

"Learn all you can, boy. You may end up farming someday."

"No, not me, unless I can farm like Papa Nels," Bobby said, using the new name for his adoptive father. "I've had enough of pigs. What I really want to do is box."

"Box, huh? You won't have any brains left by the time you're my age. But you have lots of time to figure it out." Senor chuckled.

"Do you know who bought my parents' farm, Senor Henry? There sure is a lot of work going on there. It's all painted a creamy yellow, and the buildings aren't falling down anymore. It looks good."

"Sí, I noticed. Too bad I couldn't come up with the money to buy it. It is the perfect size, the farm I've dreamed about."

"Really? Did you ever check into buying it?"

"I did out of curiosity, but the estate lawyer said it had already been sold to an anonymous buyer. He was not at liberty to say who the firm is that purchased it."

"A firm?" Bobby quizzed.

"That's what he said. I asked Nels about it, and he told me he'd heard pretty much the same information." He put the truck into gear as the line started to move forward.

"Whoever bought it must want more than the land since they're fixing the house and buildings up. What would you raise on your farm, Senor Henry?"

"Goats," he answered.

Bobby smiled. "Why goats?"

Before he could answer, someone rapped on the window.

"What's going on?" Henry asked, after having rolled the window down.

"We're closing in an hour and there's all these loads ahead of you. I'm making the cutoff here."

The man peering into the truck was the same fellow who had given Henry trouble last year.

"That hardly seems fair. They usually make exceptions toward the end of harvest when the weather forces the farmers into action," Henry said to the man.

"You might as well turn around and go home, mister."

When the man started to walk away, Henry called after him, "What about the two guys behind me? Shouldn't you tell them too?"

"Nah," he said, leaning back into the window. "They've got soybeans. Plenty of room for soybeans. The corn bins are almost full."

Bobby spouted off, "We'll take our chances and wait it out."

"Hey, aren't you the Bengtson kid? Your pappy would climb out of his grave if he saw you keeping company with illegals."

"Well, I have a new dad now, and Mr. Morales is not an illegal. He's more American than the likes of you, Gabe Ingersoll. He's—"

"Hush, Bobby," Henry demanded. Then he turned and said to the man Bobby called Gabe, "Before I go, sir, I'd like to speak to my boss. He's farther up the line."

"Fine with me," Gabe said with a snicker.

Henry exited the truck and marched past the other waiting vehicles, Gabe following behind him.

Nels's was the next wagon at the front to be weighed and unloaded. He stepped down from the tractor as Henry approached. "How far back are you, Henry?"

"Just turned the corner at the back; two other loads behind us. I was told to go home by this fellow," he said, gesturing toward Gabe.

"Why?" Nels asked, giving Gabe the stink eye.

Gabe hesitated before he answered, as if searching for a convincing reason. "It'll be dark before his turn comes, and the bins are filling fast."

"So?" Nels's evil eye never wavered as Gabe looked down and shuffled his feet. "It happens this time every year," Nels continued. "I think you're trying to cause trouble with my man just like last year."

"Oh no, Mr. Swenson. Why would I do that?"

"I don't know. You tell me," Nels replied. "Just be aware that it has been discussed at the grange meetings. If there are too many complaints by the farmers who hire migrant workers, then you're out of a job."

"I ain't heard no such talk. I've been doing this job for five years and never had no trouble," said Gabe.

"Who gives you orders to make decisions about who gets paid what or who gets to go first in line?" Nels asked.

"I answer to the co-op board of supervisors, but I'm my own man. They've never been unhappy with my work."

"Well, be prepared. That may soon change," Nels warned.

"Okay. Take a chance and have your way then," Gabe said, then hurried off.

Nels said, "Hop in and take the wheel, Henry. You and Mario will be next. I'll go to the back of the line with Bobby. When you get home, tell Kinley we'll be late."

Nels sat on the porch steps looking out over the barren fields. He found it hard to believe another year had passed. The crops were in, and winter was upon them once again. So much had happened in 1994 that he barely had time for anything but the crops and raising three teenage boys. He was sixty-two years old and starting to slow down, having less energy and more aches and pains. Fortunately, his sons gave him hope that Swenson Farms would endure for several more generations.

Hans and Tommy could successfully work the land. Tommy's agriculture knowledge, along with any new equipment and technology, was being passed on to Hans as the brothers worked together. A good team, those two.

And what an asset Mario had proved to be when added to the mix. Even at thirteen years of age, he made it his business to consult with Tommy on testing soil and researching weed killer chemicals and weather patterns.

It was earlier in spring that year when Mario had come to him with his concerns. "Grandpa, I tested the soil on the acres along the river and found it's depleted of the nutrients needed for healthy crops. I suggest you use it as pasture this year and let it recover. The cows will have plenty of water and will add fertilizer to the soil. Plus, the long-range weather forecast predicts heavy flooding this year."

Grandpa remembered chuckling and saying to Mario, "Tommy agrees with you. He told me the same thing."

Mario was also a constant reminder of profits and losses. Just look at how the soybean crops had thrived and the price they had brought this past year. Even if Mario were to choose another profession in the future, he would probably still act as a consultant for the Swensons' farm business.

One thing Nels was not able to see or predict was where Bobby would fit into the business. He usually gave a good day's work, but so far there was no indication Bobby wanted a future in farming. *He just needs more time. He's young. No need to push him into something still new to him.*

Nels's thoughts were interrupted as Henry came toward the porch from his mobile home behind the empty garden.

"Nels, I would like to leave early if it meets with your approval. I am what you call homesick for my family, and I would like to spend Thanksgiving with them in Texas. Baby Enrique is eight months old, and he will not know me."

"Yes, of course. Go with my blessing."

"Thank you, sir. I will leave sometime tomorrow. Is there any last-minute work that needs done?"

"No. We have all the help we need. And you know Kinley—she will have a bunch of stuff to give you before sending you off. I'll let her know."

Nels's eyes followed Henry as Henry walked away. He knew the day was coming when the Moraleses would not return. They would have their own farm soon, and it wouldn't be in Iowa, because Carmen Morales had an aversion to Iowa weather. Texas suited her just fine.

But Nels had a plan. It was too early to reveal, but it was coming together.

CHAPTER 25

Hans was ecstatic when his dad made a big announcement. It came the day after Senor Henry left.

"Now that you boys are teenagers, Kinley and I have decided you deserve some free time to pursue your personal interests, especially after all your hard work this past year," he said.

Oh, how Hans's had ached to play sports. He had the build and the stamina, and he was strong, eager, and ready to dedicate himself to any pain and suffering that would come with a vigorous team workout. However, a lack of transportation to merit a place on a team was often a problem for rural kids like him. Added to that was the responsibility of daily farm chores.

When school had started in the fall, Hans had elected last-period gym class, which allowed him to earn gym credits by working out with the junior varsity football team. He signed up immediately, loving the new opportunities junior high offered. By signing up, he could still feel part of the team and make it on the bus in time to go home.

Hans's football dreams were coming true. It was during the last game of the season in mid-November when the team came up short of players.

The coach approached Hans before Hans got on the bus. "Hans, I've been watching you at practice. I usually don't play my seventh graders, but I would like you to suit up for Friday's game with the

Tigers. We're two players down, and I need a good backup in case another gets injured. What do you say?"

Hans did not hesitate to accept. "Yes, sir. I'll be there."

After a short lecture about asking parental permission before committing to anything, his father dropped him off at the stadium.

"Here's your big chance, Son. Keep your mind on the game and your eye on the ball. I am proud of you. I'll be watching. Good luck."

As his dad reached out for a hug, Hans said, "Thanks, Dad. Later." He jumped out of the truck, joining the others filing into the locker room.

The coach finally found a uniform that would fit Hans from the senior varsity's equipment room. Once suited in the black and white colors, Hans felt a sense of belonging wash over him. *I may not even play tonight, but Hans Swenson is on the field.*

He huddled with the team, listening carefully to the coach's instructions, taking every word to heart. The game was the only thing on his mind even though he had sat on the bench for the first three quarters.

With only seconds left in the last quarter, the coach motioned Hans onto the ten-yard line as another team member hobbled off.

Junior high games always preceded the varsity football games. The cheerleaders and band were already gathered in their places and set the mood as Hans stepped onto the field. It didn't matter to him that his team was three points behind; he was finally playing. His job was to protect the quarterback. *I can do this. I'll show them.*

A drumroll, mixed with the roar of the crowd, increased the tension. The ball was hiked into play, and suddenly the field was a mix of jumbled school colors—orange and gold, black and white.

Where the biggest Tiger on the rival team had come from was beyond Hans's perception. The Tiger tackled the Eagle quarterback, and as the quarterback crashed to the ground, he sent a wild pass in Hans's direction.

Although it was just nanoseconds, the pass seemed to play out in slow motion as Hans reached out toward the white-stitched dimpled brown object that was about to make contact with his hand. His grip on the ball was deadly once it was secure in his hand. He made a dash for the goalposts.

From the corner of his eye, he saw a scrawny Tiger running alongside him, grabbing at his arm. The little dude was fast but not strong. Hans shifted the ball to his other hand and strong-armed the kid, sending him into a tuck-and-roll tumble.

The Tiger clinging to Hans's left leg was dragged across the finish line into the end zone.

The buzzer sounded, and the scoreboard changed: Tigers 27, Eagles 30. Hans's team had won the game.

A delirious crowd rushed onto the field and swooped Hans up, smothering him with heroic attention. He could see his mom, his dad, Mario, and Bobby stepping off the bleachers to join in. Raising his hands over his head, he made victory signs with his fingers as he waved in their direction.

The ride home after the game continued with excitement.

"Dad, the coach wants me on the junior varsity team next year. Do you think we can work it out? I've never felt so thrilled in my whole life."

"All thirteen and a half years of your life, huh?" Nels teased. "We'll see."

"And, Dad, wrestling practice starts next week. I'd sure like to try out. Please, Dad. It will be over by the end of February. I really want this, Dad."

"Whoa! Hold on there, boy. It's a bad time of year to be running you back and forth. The roads can be slick and dangerous, and the cows still need to be milked and fed. In another year you'll be able to get a permit to drive to school."

"I'm fourteen, Papa Nels," Bobby chimed in on the conversation. "Can I get a permit? Then we could stay for activities after school."

There was a pause before Nels said, "Let me think about it."

While the family was gathered around the dinner table the next evening, Mario brought up the subject they had discussed on their way home after the big win the night before.

"Grandpa, I've taught Bobby everything I can with the equipment we have in the barn. He's very good and a fast learner, but I think he could be even better with an actual ring and partners closer to his weight division for sparring."

"And?" said Grandpa.

"And maybe if Hans gets signed up for wrestling, Bobby and I could go to the gym in Ames and join the boxing club for kids our age. It would be more professional instruction. It's just a few blocks from the school."

"Yeah," said Bobby. "Can I get the permit to drive? Then you wouldn't have to bother with us when you're busy."

"Cool idea," said Hans, setting down his fork and leaning into the conversation. "Everybody wins."

"Kinley and I have already talked it over and decided to let Bobby get a license to legally drive to school. But there will be my rules in addition to the permit laws. As long as you follow the rules, it should work out, but any infractions, and your privileges will be pulled."

"What kind of rules?" Mario asked.

"Number one, if the weather becomes bad while you're in school, you're to stay put or ride the bus home. I don't want you driving in any kind of inclement weather. Number two, your route is to school and school only. Number three, no other passengers besides Mario and Hans are allowed in the car when you're driving. And number four, Bobby, if I hear you are driving too fast or not stopping at stop signs, railroad crossings, et cetera, your permit is gone. Understood?"

"Yes, sir," the three said in unison.

"We're trusting you to be mature, responsible young boys. You're good kids. Let's keep it that way," Kinley added.

Mario and the other two boys enjoyed this newfound freedom. He and Bobby coordinated their visits to the boxing gym with Hans's wrestling practice.

There were several times, though, when Hans had talked Bobby into letting him drive from the school gym to the boxing club. "Your practice runs longer than mine. I don't want to hang around the school waiting," he said.

"The club's only a couple of blocks. You can just walk down," Mario told him.

"Then I'd have to walk back with you to get the car. I'm so tired after wrestling practice. It takes a lot out of me," Hans replied.

"Yeah, and the boxing club has vending machines," Bobby chided.

"So, I get hungry too. Why are you guys making it such a big deal?"

Mario knew breaking trust with his grandpa would affect them all, so he became the conscience of the group. After several other incidents with Hans driving the car and switching drivers with Bobby about a mile from home, he threatened to tell Grandpa if it continued. This declaration earned him the nicknames "tattletale" and "snitch."

As Bobby bonded more and more with Hans, Mario saw his own relationship with Bobby dwindle. He first noticed it in the boxing ring when they were paired for sparring. Bobby acted more aggressive than usual; his punches were brutal and hurtful as if he were getting even for the threats to tell on him and Hans. *Am I imagining this, or is it for real?* Mario wondered.

By the end of February, it became obvious that Bobby was moving ahead of Mario. Bobby's reflexes, concentration, and footwork made for a powerful trio against every sparring partner, no matter their age or size. The student had advanced ahead of his first teacher and gained praise from the new trainer and their fellow boxing club members. Bobby had found his niche. He had an intense fire within him to win, to challenge, and to be a champion.

Mario remembered how his own love for boxing developed as he worked out with his father; how boxing had grown into a sport he could actually participate in without being overcome with asthma attacks; and how his boxing had built strength in his lungs and muscles.

Although Mario loved the sport and what it had done for him, he didn't want to make a career out of it or compete for awards. *Where do I fit into this world? I have so many interests. I love the farm, but farming is not for me. I see traveling like my dad in my future, seeing the world, visiting exotic places, sampling different cultures. Yeah, that's what I want to do. How do I prepare for that?*

CHAPTER 26

In early March, Mario came home alone on the bus to work on his science project rather than going to the gym with Bobby.

A large semi was backed up by the garden. The Moraleses' mobile home had been jacked up and transferred to the flatbed trailer behind it, leaving a gaping vacancy where Lupita's home had been. Mario's grandpa and Farmer Johnson were talking with the drivers.

"What's going on, Grandpa?"

"The Johnsons bought the mobile home."

"I'm confused. Where will Senor Henry and his family stay? Aren't they coming back this year?"

"They'll be here, but they will need a bigger place. The trailer was okay for the three of them, but there was no room for a baby. I'll have something ready before they come back."

"Oh, good. You had me worried," Mario said with relief.

"What brings you home so early?" Grandpa asked.

"The annual science fair in Des Moines is in two weeks. I've been working on underground temperatures and the preservation of food, a setup like the ones the pioneers used. Lots of kids my age wouldn't know how to live without modern appliances."

"Sounds interesting, but I wouldn't want to go back in time," Mr. Johnson commented.

"But everyone needs to know in case of an emergency," Mario argued.

"I think we're ready to roll out," the truck driver said, reaching over to shake hands with Grandpa. Climbing into the truck, he hollered out, "Meet you at the other end, Mr. Johnson."

The procession moved slowly away, led by Mr. Johnson, with Grandpa bringing up the rear.

Mario ate a quick snack, did a few chores, and gathered several items for his project. It was a balmy day for March. Windy hadn't been ridden much through the winter. The canvas tote bag Mario hung over the saddle horn contained a variety of produce his grandma kept out in the cool dairy barn.

The smell of melting snow blended with sunshine on the soil's surface was a fresh reminder that spring was on the way. Ascending the uphill drive of the Bengtson place, Mario saw his grandpa's truck parked near the house. *I assumed Grandpa was following Mr. Johnson home. I wonder what he's doing here.*

He dismounted Windy and walked her to the back of the house, tethering her to the rusty well pump next to the root cellar. Peering through the window of the kitchen door, he saw his grandpa standing on a ladder and painting the kitchen ceiling. *Hmm. Do I want to disturb him, or should I leave and pretend I didn't see him?*

Not wanting to make another trip, Mario decided to take the items he had brought for his project down into the cave and then leave. *That music on the radio is so loud, he won't even know I'm here.*

He unpacked the canvas bag and arranged a variety of root vegetables (potatoes, carrots, and turnips), some apples, and a large block of ice on a decaying wooden table. After comparing the items left in the cave weeks ago with the ones from the cool dairy, he wrote a few notes on their appearance, noting any that were shriveled, starting to get soft, still solid, or rotting. Then he climbed back out into the sunlight.

Grandpa's boots and overalls were the first things he saw before his head poked out.

"Mario, what the heck are you doing?"

He was so startled that he could hardly put a sentence together. "Uh … uh … I'm working on my project. I didn't want to bother you."

"You're wondering why I'm here, huh?" his grandfather asked.

Mario was unable to look his grandfather in the eye, but he was able to say sheepishly, "Well, yeah."

"Can I trust you to keep a secret? Only your grandma and I know about this."

"I promise I won't tell, Grandpa. Cross my heart and hope to die. Stick a needle in my eye."

His grandfather laughed. "That won't be necessary. It will all come out soon enough anyway. I bought the Bengtson place. It is now part of Swenson Farms. I'm fixing it up for Senor Henry's family to live in. I also have an ulterior motive. I want Senor Henry to stay in Iowa and farm the land with us. Mrs. Morales hates the Iowa climate, but if I make the place comfortable enough, maybe we can change her mind. What do you think?"

Mario's aura of suspicion had left. "That's a fantastic idea, Grandpa. Fantastic!"

"It's a perfect setup. They will have plenty of room to raise their family, and Henry's dream of having his own farm will be fulfilled."

Mario could hardly contain his delight at the prospect. "I think Lupita will be very happy. I can't wait to see her reaction."

"Remember, you're not to breathe a word of this to Hans or Bobby, especially Bobby," said Grandpa. "I may change the arrangements if it upsets him."

"Bobby really likes Senor Henry. I think it will be a great surprise. How long will it be before they come?" Mario said.

"Could be as early as April, but they will probably wait until Lupita's school is over if she and Carmen plan to come with him."

"Grandpa, what if they don't show up? What happens then?"

His grandfather dismissed the thought. "Don't even go there. Think positive, Mario."

Mario sat on the porch with Grandpa and Tommy that same evening, and Tommy also was made aware of Grandpa's secret.

"Yeah, I needed to tell you, Tommy, because decisions have to be made right away. Mario knows because he caught me there this afternoon. But the other boys don't know," said Grandpa.

"Will you wait for Henry's return? Or should we start working the land?" Tommy asked.

"Well, Henry's free to plant what he likes. I'm just concerned that he'll be back late this year. Let's go ahead and plant soybeans there."

The following Sunday after church, the doorbell rang just as Papa Nels finished saying grace, and Kinley began passing the brussels sprouts. Bobby seized the opportunity and hopped up to answer the door before the evil little cabbages could reach his spot at the table.

"You still have to eat some," Kinley yelled after him.

Bobby recognized the familiar figure through the sheer curtains on the door. What a welcome sight to see Senor's thick mustache, beat-up straw hat, and easygoing slouch as he stood with one hand propped on his hip.

Bobby shouted toward the others as he unlatched the door: "It's Senor Henry!"

There was the sound of chairs pushing away from the table and the rush of feet coming to greet the awaited farmhand. The whole family was filled with delight at the announcement.

"Where is the rest of your family?" Mario asked, peering past Senor Henry toward the empty truck.

Senor leaned against the doorway and pointed to the vacant spot behind the garden. "I have a bigger question: Where is the trailer? Did you not expect me this year?"

"Come in, Henry, and sit down." Papa Nels motioned him to the table. "Yes, we were expecting you. About the mobile home: I've made other arrangements. We'll talk about that after we eat."

Kinley laid a plate in front of the newly arrived guest. "Will Carmen and the children come this year?" she asked.

"They will come later, after Lupita finishes school," Senor Henry answered. "Carmen has a driver's license and a van now, but she will need a place to live," he added, speaking a little bit louder and shooting a dumbfounded look at Papa Nels.

"I've got it all worked out, Henry."

Bobby noticed the eye contact and the smiles that passed between his new parents and Mario. He leaned next to Mario's ear and whispered, after he had punched his leg under the table, "What do you know?"

"Ouch. I'm not telling," Mario whispered back.

"Does Hans know too?" Bobby said under his breath with his teeth gritted.

"What's going on over there?" Papa Nels asked, addressing the two boys.

"Bobby snuck his brussels sprouts onto my plate," Mario lied.

"Did not," Bobby said.

Kinley rolled her eyes. "Henry, do you see what you're in for? How is little Henry? I bet he is growing up fast. I can't wait to hold him."

Senor smiled and said proudly, "Oh, he is a handful already. He was starting to walk before I left."

Bobby inflicted a kick to Mario's foot this time as the adults talked. "You didn't answer my question. Am I the only one who doesn't know what Papa Nels has planned?"

"No."

"No what?" Bobby pressed.

Mario said in his normal voice, "Hans doesn't know."

Hans stopped eating for a second. "I heard my name. What don't I know?"

Papa Nels held up his hands. "Enough. Kinley, I guess we need to make the announcement before dessert if we want any peace around here."

"I can eat and listen," Hans stated.

"Hush," Kinley said to her son.

Papa Nels laid down his fork and took a sip of coffee. "Henry, I'm the one who bought the Bengtson property. It is now part of Swenson Farms."

Bobby stared, his mouth hanging open.

"Bobby," Papa Nels continued, "I wasn't sure how you would feel about what I did. I was going to tell you before Henry arrived, but as you see, he came earlier than I anticipated. I fixed the place up for the Moraleses to live in. The trailer would not have been comfortable for their growing family."

Senor Henry's smile said it all. "Oh, Nels, that is too kind. We would have managed in the trailer."

"Knowing you, Henry, you would have made it work, but I was hoping you would want to stay on permanently and sharecrop with us. How do you feel about that, Bobby?"

Still in shock when everyone turned to look at him, Bobby stammered, "Will it be Senor Henry's farm or yours, Papa Nels?"

"Henry will be a partner. I paid the back taxes and a few other bills, in addition to purchasing the land. Henry will operate it as his farm and pay for it from our profits on crops and livestock."

"Maybe Bobby will want to farm someday," Senor Henry ventured.

"Oh no," Bobby said without hesitation.

"You are young and may change your mind in time," Senor said.

"The price I paid for the land will be put into a trust for Bobby," said Papa Nels.

Henry put his hand over Bobby's hand, which was resting on the table, "So, you will be okay with this arrangement?"

"Just one request, Senor Henry." Bobby picked up his fork and waved it as he shouted, "No pigs please!"

Even Hans laughed as he finished off the last piece of chicken on the platter.

"There is only one question that remains," Papa Nels said. "How will Carmen feel about this?"

CHAPTER 27

After Sunday dinner, Henry toured his new dwelling with Nels. "Oh, this is nice. You have done a lot of work. The ladies can't help but love it—lots of room, modern appliances, big closets for storage, and plenty of space for a garden." His eyes wandered around the premises as he spoke. His mind was already made up to stay, and he was determined to convince Carmen.

"Check this out," said Nels, opening a door to the nursery. It was decorated with ponies and cowboys.

"Oh, that is too cute. Carmen will have no problem living here. Did you know I put a bid on the place a few weeks after they found Mr. Bengtson's body? When did you buy it, Nels?"

"Since it borders on Swenson property, I didn't hesitate to scoop it up. I wanted to buy it years ago before the Bengtsons moved in, but I couldn't come up with the money then. What do you plan to grow here? Tommy and I thought we'd let you decide."

"Well, Bobby doesn't want to see pigs here." He laughed. "He made fun of me when I said I'd like to raise goats, but I like goats. I'll start with a pair or two and see what happens. If everyone is in agreement, I'd like to grow some alfalfa and hay for my goats."

Nels smiled and said, "It's your decision, Henry. I like the idea of goats. I've had several requests over time for goat milk. Once you get started, we can add it to our line of dairy products."

"My little Enrique has been raised on goat milk. He loves it. Many babies can't tolerate regular cow's milk."

Nels shook his hand. "Sounds like we're off to a good start. You can pick out your goats anytime and charge them to Swenson Farms."

As the two men headed to look through the barn, Mario and Bobby rode up on Windy.

Bobby slid down and followed them. "I can't believe the old farm could look this great, Senor."

"Remarkable," Henry agreed. "Why are you riding with Mario on his horse? Where is Ebony?"

"I wasn't sure I should ride him yet. It hasn't even been a year since the doc fixed his leg."

"I figured you'd have at least started training him. You won't be using him as a racehorse or a workhorse. A little guy like you could get up on him soon. He's nearly two years. The leg should be mended by now. Would you like some help getting started?"

Bobby said emphatically, "I just didn't want to hurt him."

Henry, in a caring manner, drew Bobby to his side. "Tell you what. I'll be over later this evening and take a look at Ebony's leg. If everything seems okay, we'll start training him with a bridle."

"Thanks. That makes me feel better," said Bobby.

Mario caught up with them as they entered the barn.

"I haven't done any work in here, Henry, but you'll need some stalls for your goats," Nels said.

Bobby smiled at Henry. "You're really getting goats?"

Henry laughed and nodded. "Sí. I'll never have to mow the place. It's another advantage of having goats."

"Hans, Bobby, and I can help build stalls, right, Bobby?" said Mario.

Bobby stopped walking and, completely out of the blue, as if the thought had just hit him, said to Senor, "Now that you have your own farm, Senor, will you want Ebony back?"

"Who do you think I am? Ebony is your horse, Bobby. I'm a man of my word."

Bobby let out a sigh of relief. His smile returned. "Boy, am I glad to hear that. I figured I'd have to camp out in your barn just to see him."

They hurried past the area where the pigs and Mr. Bengtson had died as if none of them wanted to linger, converse, or traipse through the area.

Henry scratched his head, looking at the root cellar cave. "What will I do with this? With your approval, Nels, maybe I can fill it in and make it part of Carmen's garden."

Mario protested immediately, saying, "No, no, Senor Henry. It's good for storing taters and other root vegetables way into winter. I just won third place at the science fair for my research on preserving produce like the pioneers used to do."

"That's a new one to me," said Henry. "We do not use caves in Mexico or the southern United States because we do not have harsh winters. We can grow hot peppers and chilies year-round," he said, grinning.

"You'll see how handy it will be," said Mario.

"Okay, I will leave the cave."

Henry playfully cuffed Bobby's ears as they wound up their jaunt around his new property. "How's the boxing coming along?"

"Aw, it's okay, but I can't do the footwork properly because of the toes that were amputated. My trainer says I'll have to develop my own style of balance because of it."

"Oh, he's just being modest," Mario said. "He's the best in spite of missing toes."

"Are you boys ready to go home?" Nels asked after they had finished the tour. "Henry, come join us for supper."

Henry dismissed them with a wave of his hand. "You all go ahead. I'll come later. I have many things to think about, and Carmen sent a lot of food that I need to finish."

Bobby climbed up on Windy's back behind Mario. "Goodbye, Senor. See you later. Don't forget."

"Remember, I'm a man of my word," he called after them.

Henry watched until they were out of sight before he moved. *What a blessing to see young Bobby thriving since being placed in the Swenson family.* It was his intention for Ebony to be Bobby's horse right from the start. After seeing and hearing of the harsh treatment Bobby had suffered at his father's hands, Henry knew it was love and understanding that Bobby needed, rather than anger and cruelty. Bobby's remarks and meanness toward Henry and his daughter, Lupita, were a product of his father's domineering hatred. And Bobby's need for acceptance and attention, as well as his need to fit in, even if it was with the wrong kind of people, came from his father's lack of concern for the boy.

Ebony was like Bobby, broken, unwanted, and having no potential for a bright future given the way things were. But together, the boy and animal began to heal in a good environment at the Swensons'. Ebony was spared to help save another, namely, a young boy named Bobby Bengtson.

Bobby's rescue from the frozen snow and the scars left by a cruel father had changed Henry's heart and mind toward the boy, and he had pledged to make it his mission to aid in Bobby's recovery. In pursuit of that mission, Henry had crossed paths with a man who planned to destroy a deformed colt that also held little value in his master's eyes.

No, Bobby, I won't forget. It does my soul good to see you and Ebony alive and happy.

CHAPTER 28

It was a peaceful evening in early June. School was out for the summer; seeds were germinating in the ground, ready to pop into crops; and the boys were taking their evening ride after supper, which usually took them in the direction of Senor Henry's casa.

Each time Bobby mounted his shiny black horse, it was as exhilarating as the first time Ebony had let him ride. The transition had gone smoothly because of the trust the two had built over the past year. There was no resistance or bucking. Bobby had felt welcomed when he climbed on Ebony's bare back and nudged him to a slow trot. Ebony's scars were healed and covered, leaving no one to suspect he had ever been anything but perfect.

Sitting high above the others on his horse was a day that would be etched in Bobby's mind forever. He felt proud and important as he pranced his beautiful horse past the front porch, waving to Papa Nels and Mom Kinley. Ebony was definitely a showstopper.

Since Bobby, Hans, and Mario had helped organize the barn and install the goat pens, Bobby was anxious to see the goats Senor and Papa Nels had bought at the livestock auction that morning.

"How many old goats did they buy?" Hans asked as they rode.

Mario spoke up, "Grandpa said four."

"Yeah. Lupita gets to name them, and they're not old," Bobby added. "One of them is pregnant."

"Ooh, goody," said Hans with an eye roll. "I hate goat meat. I hope we're not expected to eat them. Yuk!"

"Senor Henry calls it mutton," Mario said.

"Call it whatever you like, I hate it. It's greasy and chewy."

"Papa Nels and Senor want the goats for milk. Papa plans to add goat milk products to our dairy line," Bobby said with family authority.

Senor Henry came outside as the boys noisily approached the house. "Hey, my friends. What's new?" He took hold of Ebony, tethered him to a sapling, and helped Bobby down.

"Your goats, that's what's new," said Mario. "We came to see them."

"I just finished milking the two females. Would you like to try some of the milk? You'll grow to love it."

"Pass," said Hans, still astride Buck.

"I'd like to try some," Mario said, climbing down from Windy.

"I'm not much of a pioneer," said Bobby. "I'll let Mario test it first."

A green van with Texas license plates pulled up the drive as they were debating.

"Por dios! My family has arrived," Senor shouted.

A young woman jumped from the passenger side of the van and ran toward Senor. He scooped her up in his arms and swung her around, her loose dark hair flying around her face.

Bobby's eyes bugged out. His mouth was agape. He nudged Mario and whispered, "Is that Lupita?" It had been a couple of years since he'd last seen her.

Mario nodded as if in a trance himself.

Hans made a soft whistle under his breath and carved an hourglass shape in the air in front of his saddle.

Bobby gulped back a guilty lump in his throat, recalling the cruel things he had done and said to Senor Henry's daughter. *Oh man! How will I make that right? Does she remember? Will she ever forgive me? Why does she look so different?*

Lupita's grown-up look was startling. Her thick shiny tresses matched the sheen of Ebony's black coat. All Bobby could remember from before was the straggling hair escaping from her ponytail or braids and gathering around her face. The snug jeans and T-shirt she was wearing emphasized certain areas of her once nondescript stick figure. What happened to the sassy girl he once had taunted with meanness?

Mario froze as Lupita came close to him, after Senor had put her down. He stood wooden and speechless as she reached out and gave him a hug.

She pushed back from him, holding him at arm's length, and said, "Aren't you glad to see me?"

Mario allowed for a few seconds of hesitation before he stammered, "Uh … yes. It's … it's just that you've changed so much."

She laughed and playfully punched his arm. "No I haven't."

That made him soften a little, and he initiated the next hug. Being so close to her, his nostrils were filled with the scent of the red flowers of summer, fresh like peonies and geraniums, sweet like dainty roses, and overpowering like the stargazer lily, beckoning him to linger longer.

Lupita suddenly broke away and dashed off to help Mrs. Morales unload the van. Mario still felt breathless minutes later.

Hans had dismounted Buck after smoothing the top and sides of his crew cut, anticipating a generous embrace from Lupita too. Alas, he was left holding Buck's reins, having been totally ignored by the lovely Lupita.

Senor called out while unloading the van, "Don't just stand there, guys. Let's help the ladies carry some of this stuff. You can set it on the porch until Carmen knows where she wants it put."

Balancing Enrique on her hip, Carmen shouted from the front porch, "Come, Henry. I want to see inside. It is so different from the house we used to drive by."

"Do you like it so far?" he asked as he approached.

"Yes, as long as we're gone before the snow flies."

He chuckled and gave her a kiss. "I was hoping you'd like to stay on. Just look at that big garden waiting to be planted. And the barn has four goats and one on the way. Think of all the time we will save not driving and moving every six months. Lupita will not have to disrupt her studies or leave her friends." He figured he might as well start his campaign early to entice her to commit.

"I promise to think it over, but no agreement yet."

"That's all I ask for now," he said, opening the door to the house.

"Oh, this must be Ebony," Lupita said to Bobby when she spotted the horse tethered next to the porch. "Papa told me all about him." She set a box of clothing down and ran to admire the sleek beauty.

"Yep, that's him. Did he also tell you about me?" Bobby asked.

"Yes. I know your circumstances, Bobby. I'm sorry about your parents, but you have a good home now."

"Listen, Lupita, I'm sorry for all the bad names I called you and for breaking your arm when you fell off Mario's horse." He started to say more, but she stopped him with a gentle touch of his arm.

"That's all in the past. I forgive you, if you promise never to do anything like that again. Okay?"

"Scout's honor," he responded. "You want to ride Ebony? He's very gentle."

"Sure. But I must help Mama and Papa get us settled first." She nuzzled Ebony's neck and laid her cheek against his soft snout. "I'll be back later," she whispered.

"One more thing, Lupita. You have to see the goats. Your father waited for you to name them."

"Really? Oh, I have to see them. I can't wait a minute longer." Bobby was close behind her as she ran toward the barn.

Lupita stopped momentarily and looked back when she heard the sound of hoofbeats galloping down the driveway. It was Hans.

"Where's he going?" she shouted back to Mario.

"Beats me!" Mario answered as he set down a large box on the porch.

I know the reason he left. He's jealous because Lupita didn't give him the attention he expected. I have to say, I'm feeling a little perturbed right now too. Why does she find Bobby so interesting?

CHAPTER 29

Henry started to fret. The goats, which Lupita had named Mammy, Pappy, Billy, and Nanny, were a constant torture to Carmen. They ate everything in their path, including her garden, the shrubbery, tree limbs within their reach, and clothes off the clothesline.

"It is like having four more children to keep an eye on," she wailed to Henry. "Pappy is the worst. I have nearly worn out my broom whacking his furry butt. He gets into more trouble than the others combined. Even when I stake them in the yard, they manage to chew through the ropes," she cried.

"I'm sorry, dear," he said, rethinking his idea to buy goats and concluding it was not a good decision.

"Today they chased the chickens and ducks. The only way I could control them was to sic Gonzales the rooster on them like a dog. They're afraid of him. That was my day. You have to help me, Henry. I can't live like this."

"Can you hang in there awhile longer, dear? I'll talk with Nels about putting in some fences." *Boy, I need to remedy this pronto. I don't want to lose my dream over some ornery goats. I think Carmen likes it here otherwise.*

"They will just chomp down the fences too. I swear, they have iron bellies. The baby, Sunshine, is a jumper. She likes to stand up on the cave and bleat for attention, then she'll jump off and run if Lupita or I try to catch her. It is a game with her. I'm fighting a losing battle, Henry," she continued to agonize.

"Now, now, calm down. Promise me you'll give me a chance to fix things," he said, stroking her cheek.

She nodded. "Okay, but I'm not sure it will be enough to keep me here."

Henry wore a long face that afternoon as he joined Nels in the dairy barn.

"What's wrong, Henry? More trouble with the goats?"

"Yes. Carmen was so upset this morning that I didn't bother to tell her about Pappy gnawing off the corner of the rear license plate on the van. My intentions were good, Nels, but I'm not sure things will work out. How soon before I have to sign the final papers on the farm?" he said downheartedly.

"Don't worry about the papers. Maybe this will help." Nels held several documents up in front of Henry. "We have two new clients who want the goat milk."

Henry felt a smile crease his lips. It was the best news he had had all day. "Really?!"

Nels slapped him on the back. "Yep. I think once word gets out, we'll have even more."

Henry continued to smile as he thought for a few seconds. "Then I would like to take time off to put in some fences back behind the house where the goats can romp and graze without bothering Carmen."

"Well, why didn't you say so? Don't just stand there. Let's go! We'll convince her yet, Henry." Nels chuckled. "I'll get the boys. We'll meet you at the lumberyard in town."

"Okay! I'll start by ordering lots of barbwire." He laughed.

In the next two weeks, Henry, Nels, and the three boys secured fence posts in the holes Tommy had dug with his auger, then they worked on stringing the wire. The first fence enclosure, gates and all, was completed within one week. Once the two other areas were finished, Henry's life became more content because Carmen had grown more at ease.

"Oh, Henry, just look at how the garden thrives. And I no longer worry about leaving the baby's toys and my baskets outside. Now I can string the hammock between the two trees in front and hang the laundry on the clothesline without keeping an eye on it." She pulled a towel off the line and handed it to him. "Doesn't it smell delightful? Like sunshine and fresh air. Now this is living," she said.

"Dear Carmen, are you giving me hope that you will stay?"

"I think we should let Lupita in on this decision too, Henry."

"I'm right here, Mama, Papa," Lupita called, leaning over the rail of the front porch, several feet away from where they stood.

"Chica, you have been listening all this time?"

"Yes, Papa. This is my home. I always hate to leave Iowa. I will miss my abuela though. She is getting so old. What will she do if we don't return to Texas?"

"I have been thinking about that," said Carmen. "There is still an unused room off the living area. I wonder if Nels would allow us to bring her here."

"Oh yes! A perfect idea, Mama. Senor Nels is a very kind man. I also know from Bobby that he would do anything to keep you here, Papa. Don't wait too long to decide, Mama. We will need what's left of summer to get Grandmama settled," Lupita said.

Henry was all grins and giggles just knowing Carmen had been thinking of staying. "You are right, Chica. Nels will need to know soon. What do you say, dear? Can we make it official?"

"Sí."

With all his might, Henry swung Carmen around the yard, laughing and kissing her chubby tan cheeks.

Hans was concerned about his plans for the upcoming school year because the last part of summer was going to be hectic for everyone now that Carmen had agreed to stay in Iowa. Bobby was going with the Moraleses to Texas to help with the grandmother's move. Kinley and Tommy's wife, Peg, had offered to watch little Enrique while they were gone. Mario would be with his other grandparents in Myanmar to visit Aunt Cherise the last week of July and the first two weeks of August.

When the opportunity arose, Hans asked for a few things he wanted in return for taking on extra chores. "Dad, I know you have a lot going on, and I'm willing to help out, but if I had a driver's permit, you wouldn't have to drive me to football practice three times a week. You promised I could join the team this year."

"Hans …"

"You promised, Dad. It's not fair that I always get left behind to do all the work, milking those freaky goats, cleaning up their messes, and getting them to pasture each day. Not fair at all."

"It's only for a short time, Hans."

"When does my turn come to have fun or do something I like for a change?" The look on his father's face told Hans he was winning, so he exaggerated his dejected expression by making his bottom lip quiver a little as he talked and occasionally wiped at his eyes.

"Save the theatrics, Son. If you think you can handle both the chores and football practice, we'll go get that driver's permit. Okay?"

"Thanks, Dad," Hans exclaimed with a drastic change of expression.

CHAPTER 30

Henry returned to Iowa five days later with his mother-in-law in tow. After dropping off Bobby, introducing Carmen's mother to the Swensons, and collecting young Enrique, the Moraleses headed to their new home for a good night's rest.

The next morning, Henry met Nels in the dairy barn at eight o'clock with a canister of goat milk for their first client. "Good morning, Nels. It is good to be home."

"We're glad you're back too, especially Hans." Nels chuckled.

"I hope there weren't any problems."

"Nothing serious. The baby goat got over the fence one morning. Hans watched the little bugger stand on the slope on the north pasture and jump right over the fence. Actually, I believe he found it amusing. He caught her and staked her in the area. You're going to have to keep an eye on that one."

"Yes, I forgot to warn Hans about her. Sorry."

"Henry, are you ready to go over our contract once more and make any changes before you sign the final documents?"

"About that, Nels. There is something I must tell you. I should have done it before I brought my mother-in-law here to live. You may have a change of heart about taking me on as a partner."

"What could be so bad that I would do that?" Nels asked seriously, while he filled a couple of mugs with coffee from the pot in the dairy office. He set them on the small desk, then motioned for Henry to sit down with him.

Henry, with his head hung, felt his shoulders droop as he began. "Well, sir, do you remember when Bobby's slingshot caused Lupita to have a broken arm when she fell off the horse? I wanted to confront the kid face-to-face, but you asked me to hold my anger, and I abided by your wishes. But when school started up again in the fall, it was obvious Bobby had not changed or learned a lesson, so I decided to do things my way by confronting him and his parents."

Nels leaned back in his chair, his arms folded across his chest. "I'm listening, my friend."

"When I started up their driveway, I saw an official car there from Story County Public Schools and backed out. Before I headed back to the farm, I noticed the gate to our south field across the road was open, so I stopped and pulled in to shut it, only to find it had a loose hinge that prevented it from closing. As I got my tools out to fix it, the car at the Bengtsons' house left.

"I waited a few minutes trying to decide what to do, but my anger at Bobby was still eating away at my soul. So, I walked across the road, thinking about what I would say as I marched back up their drive.

"I could hear the ruckus going on inside before I reached the front steps. The way the Bengtsons were carrying on stopped me from rapping on the door. The screaming, crying, and cruel, hateful language paralyzed me.

"Peering through the screen of their open door, I saw Mr. Bengtson beating Bobby unmercifully as Mrs. Bengtson tried to pull him away. Mr. B hit her, knocking her across the room, then continued to lash Bobby with a leather riding crop and kick him at every opportunity.

"Mrs. B grabbed a log from a pile near the stove and hit her husband in the head with a force I've never seen a woman use.

"I don't know what took place before I got there, but I did see that she whispered to Bobby and sent him upstairs.

"All my previous anger had left. I felt I should have interfered and stopped Mr. Bengtson, but the damage had been done. Mrs.

Bengtson handled things well, and I applaud her for what she did. So, I quietly walked away and returned to my business of fixing the gate, but I was really shaken by what I had witnessed."

"Wow!" Nels remarked. "Poetic justice prevailed. I'm surprised you kept this from me."

"There is more," Henry said. He took a sip of coffee and continued. "I was about finished with the gate when Bengtson's truck came barreling down the driveway, leaving a cloud of white rock dust behind. As his truck approached the road, there were shots fired. I could see the dusty figure of Mr. Bengtson running after the truck. Bobby was driving, and Mrs. Bengtson was sitting on the passenger's side.

"Bobby made a sharp turn onto the road, shifted gears, and gave it some gas. Mr. Bengtson stood in the middle of the road, took aim, and fired one last time. I heard breaking glass and knew the bullet had hit the fleeing truck. He then lowered the rifle to his side, looking dejected and alone as they sped away.

"My heart cheered again for his wife and son. 'Godspeed,' I yelled out loud. 'I saw what you did to that boy and your wife, Mr. Bengtson.'

It was then he noticed me. He lifted the rifle back in position and came toward me. 'Give me the keys to your truck,' he said, the gun pointed in my face.

"I said, 'no,' because the keys were still in the truck and I didn't want him to know. Obviously, the old man wasn't thinking right and tried to strong arm me. We wrestled for the gun, but before I could get a good hold, it fired, throwing him backward on the ground. I walked over and kicked that rifle across the field out of his reach. I figured he was grazed by the bullet because a small amount of blood appeared on the left side of his shirt. But he seemed okay.

'Go ahead and finish me off,' he begged.

'Nah,' I said. 'Your troubles aren't over. I think the sheriff might be interested in what I witnessed today.'

"He laid there staring blankly at me as I got into my truck and left, but I drove slowly. Checking my rearview mirror, I saw him get up, walk over and retrieve the rifle, and make his way back across the road and up his driveway."

"Henry, you should have at least told me. He could have shot you in cold blood. And who knows what might have happened if he'd gotten in your truck and chased after Bobby and his mother," Nels said.

"I figured you would know if he called the sheriff or sent him after me. I didn't want any trouble with the law. The way some people around here treat the migrants, I wasn't sure what I'd be accused of or charged with. I was very relieved when nothing came of it."

Nels replied, "That's because Bengtson didn't want to expose his own guilt of domestic abuse and attempted murder of his own wife and kid. Of course, he also didn't have a phone or a truck, so he was stuck on the farm."

Henry shook his head. "I've agonized every day since then about how long it was before he died. Tell me, what should I do, Nels?"

"I don't think for a minute that you killed Jake Bengtson. Your fingerprints were not found on the gun, and it sounds like Mrs. Bengtson clobbered him pretty good with that log. He may have developed a blood clot on his brain from the hit, or it's possible he shot himself when you struggled. Maybe he even had a stroke from all the trauma that took place. So, please stop beating yourself up, Henry."

"Do I need to tell the sheriff what I know?" Henry asked. "It might not look good for me after waiting all this time, especially since I made an offer on the Bengtson farm right after Jake's remains were found."

A cry came from the corner of the dairy barn: "No, Senor, please don't do that." Bobby ran and threw his arms around Henry's shoulders. "Please don't," he sobbed.

"Bobby, how long have you been listening?" Nels bellowed.

"I saw Senor's truck outside and came in to see him. I heard everything. Papa Nels, don't tell the sheriff. I know Senor never did anything wrong. He is a good man. Everything he said is true about why Mom and I left. After the truant officer was gone, my pop gave me the worst beating ever. If Pop had been alive when I came back here, I'd be locked up right now for murder, because that's why I returned home. I planned to kill him for what he did to my mother. I had nothing to lose. She was the only one who ever cared about me until I met you and Senor Henry. You guys saved my life."

"Bobby, listen to me," said Nels. "The cause of your father's death is listed as unknown, and I don't believe we have anything to tell the authorities that will change the verdict. The sheriff knows your story, Bobby, and we know Henry was defending his property and himself against an armed man. Henry did not pull the trigger on the gun. We will never know for sure what your father died from. The bottom line is that Henry protected you from God knows what if your father had caught you."

"I just thought of something," said Henry. "I was wearing my work gloves at the time. They are very bulky. I would not be able to fire a weapon with them on, especially during a struggle."

"There you go," said Nels. "We have nothing to offer or gain by having the investigation reopened. Right, Bobby?"

"Yes, sir. I like the way things are."

Nels smiled. "Henry, I'm glad you told me this. Shall we go sign those papers now?"

CHAPTER 31

It was mid-August. The crops and garden were bursting with a cornucopia harvest. The Iowa State Fair had just ended, where both Bobby and Hans had been presented with ribbons of honor. Bobby won Best of Show in the two-and-under horse category for his most prized possession, Ebony, and Hans proudly accepted a blue ribbon for the dairy cow he had groomed into a champion.

Kinley prepared a dinner from their wealth of produce in anticipation of Mario's return home from Myanmar: panfried chicken, a kettle of sweet corn on the cob, cabbage slaw, roasted red potatoes, sliced tomatoes, a mix of cucumbers and onions, and baked apples.

Mario and his other grandparents called to say their flight would arrive at the Des Moines airport around five o'clock.

At six o'clock, Hans said to Bobby, as they waited on the front steps, "Where are they? I'm hungry. My guts are growling."

"Kind of like you," Bobby said with a grin.

"It's all I can do to sit here smelling cinnamon apples baking and thinking about that golden crusty skin on the fried chicken. Now my mouth is watering too. Why don't they call or something? If they're going to be late, why can't we eat and save them some?" Hans protested.

Kinley stepped out on the porch. "They're running a little late but should be here in half an hour. There was a problem collecting their luggage and a long line at the car rental. We'll eat as soon as they arrive."

Hans groaned. "Can I have a slice of bread with jam to tide me over?"

"There's a bag of carrot sticks and celery in the refrigerator if you can't wait."

Hans groaned again. "I'd rather eat chicken feed."

Bobby offered an alternative: "You want to go for a quick ride?"

"Where to?"

"Mom Kinley," Bobby said, "Would it be okay if Lupita came for dinner to welcome Mario too?"

"She's welcome anytime."

"Let's go, Hans," Bobby said, starting for the barn.

"Nah. You go. I think I'll go try some of those veggie sticks."

"Your choice," Bobby said, and left.

Mario reached over Grandpa Fontanini's shoulder from the back seat and pressed the horn all the way up the rocky drive when he saw everyone congregated on the front porch—everyone but Hans. Coming home with news from Myanmar, Mario found that it was all he could do to contain his excitement as he hugged each one.

His grandmother held him at arm's length. "Look at you. Whatever happened on your vacation must really have agreed with you. I haven't seen you this happy for a long time."

In a high-pitched voice, he said, "Didn't you get my letters?"

"We only got one letter. It was when you first arrived," she responded.

"Where's Hans? He'll want to hear this too."

"He's sitting at the table with fork and knife in hand, ready to stab into the chicken," said Grandpa Swenson, laughing and getting caught up in his grandson's excitement. "Let's move inside to the dining room and hear all about it."

After Nels had said grace, Hans, Grandpa Fontanini, Emma,

and Bobby dug into the food, but Grandma and Grandpa Swenson and Lupita sat ready to listen to the cause of his elation.

"Once we were settled at the mission where Aunt Cherise works," he began, "Cherise took us on a tour of Myanmar. We had lunch at a Thai restaurant, and afterward there were some friends she wanted us to meet before we went back to the mission clinic.

"Her friends had a really nice home for that part of the world. There were palm trees and beautiful flowers that you would have liked, Lupita, because they were all shades of red, pink, and orange."

Lupita smiled. "I can picture it in my head. Go on, tell us more."

"Cherise introduced her friend Malee, who, after a very warm greeting, ushered us into a cozy area near the hearth of her home. I recognized her right away as the woman in the picture on Dad's desk when we toured the oil rig. As my eyes wandered around the room, I spotted it immediately," said Mario, relishing the attention as his story built.

Bobby stopped with his fork midway to his mouth. "What was it?"

"At first I was surprised. Then I was curious. The more I gazed at it, the more confused I became." His smile widened as Hans joined his audience.

"I looked at Aunt Cherise, pointed at the shelf, and started to say, 'Is that …,' and she nodded, tears forming in her eyes."

"How long are you going to drag this out? Tell us!" Hans demanded.

"Malee set a tray of refreshments on the table in front of us, then she reached up and took the object of my fixation from the mantel. 'Your father, Mario. My husband,' she said."

Mario's grandmother froze. He continued: "Malee handed me the bottle containing my father's ashes that Cherise had taken back to Myanmar after Dad's funeral."

Kinley gasped. "Oh my! When did all that happen? Norman, did you know about this? Emma?" she said, looking at them.

Norman answered, "Not until I checked with Tony's lawyer

about his estate plans for Mario. Cherise told me she had introduced Malee to Tony when he was working near Myanmar and came for a visit. Malee is a very gracious lady. She is well educated and speaks fluent English with a little bit of an accent."

Mario added, "She is beautiful too. Aunt Cherise said Dad made many trips after their first introduction, and then one day they up and married. It was a few months before he wrapped up the job there and moved to the Gulf of Mexico. Their wedding was a mixed ceremony in a Burmese temple with the Christian mission pastor officiating."

"How long ago was that?" Grandpa Nels asked.

"A little over a year before he died," Grandpa Fontanini replied.

"So why didn't he tell you, Emma, and Mario that summer you spent with him in Texas?" Grandpa Nels continued to pry.

"I don't know, Nels. I too saw the woman's picture on Tony's desk, but I assumed she was a girlfriend. His attention to Mario that summer turned hectic at times: several times he was a no-show for our plans, often he was tired when we did get together, and he seemed always to have a lot on his mind. The only thing I could surmise from what Cherise and the attorney told me is that Tony planned to bring his bride to the States and introduce her after he finished the job in Corpus Christi."

Hans and Bobby went back to eating. Grandma Swenson began to pick at her food.

Mario hadn't finished his story. "But wait, you guys, you haven't heard the best part!" he shouted to bring back everyone's attention. "My dad had a good reason for being so distracted when we were in Texas. He was flying back and forth to Myanmar. Malee was expecting a baby, but the baby didn't come at the expected time. It came a week later, after Dad returned to Texas."

"Finish the story, Mario," said Grandma Emma with a smile.

"I have a baby sister. Dad named her Lindy." He beamed.

"Lindy?" said Grandma Swenson, raising her voice. "He had the audacity to name her after my daughter, Belinda?"

"Now, now, Kinley," said Nels. "Would it be so bad if he did? I think it's sweet."

"It was his pet name for my daughter. How dare he use it for his offspring with another woman?" She pushed away from the table and ran upstairs.

"What did I say wrong?" Mario asked, looking around the table. His surprise news had turned sour with this proclamation from his grandmother.

Even the food turned cold in the aftermath of the scene.

CHAPTER 32

The yellow school bus stopped at the farmhouse and shuttled the boys and Lupita off to their first day of eighth grade. Kinley rocked in her chair on the front porch with a mug of coffee, enjoying the quietude of the morning. Nine years ago, Mario started kindergarten with Hans, a few months before his mother died. For nine years, Kinley and Nels had been Mario's guardian with few visits, phone calls, or parenting guides from Tony. Without divulging any notion of the bad feelings between them and Tony, she and Nels often overlooked Tony's indiscretions, made excuses for him, or smoothed things over to protect Mario's image of his father.

It had been nearly a week since Kinley left the table in a huff after hearing about Tony Fontanini's new wife and baby.

Somewhere on another continent Mario has a little sister, Lindy. Does she resemble him in any way? She probably has dark hair and eyes, maybe darker skin if she is eastern Indian more than Asian. I know he is confused about my reaction. I have no desire to dredge up old wounds, and Nels tries to reason with me, but I just can't forget how Tony treated Belinda and their little boy.

The mailman drove up the driveway, stopped, and walked up the steps to where Kinley was sitting. "I saw you sitting here and thought you might want these," he said, handing her a pack of letters. "They look important—all of them from Burma."

"Oh yes. They're a little late, but I'm anxious to read them anyway," she said. "Thank you for bringing them to me."

"No problem," he said, lingering while she studied each one.

"They are from my grandson Mario, who spent some time there this summer with his other grandparents and an aunt who lives there. They are old news by now."

The letter carrier offered more conversation, saying, "They felt a little heavy, as if maybe there are some pictures inside. I've never been to that part of the world. Did he go on a safari?"

"I don't think so," said Kinley. "I'll read through them later and see if there's anything he forgot to tell us. Thank you again."

The letters lay in her lap unopened until the postman finally left.

She opened the letter with the oldest postmark and sorted through pictures of lotus flowers, exotic frogs, Buddhist temples and statues, and Aunt Cherise at the mission clinic. She could feel Mario's happiness with each click of the camera. The letter itself reflected the same message; he was in his element exploring new and different territory. *Belinda's little Mario, so smart, so loving, so eager to learn all about the world and its people. Perhaps he will be a world traveler.*

The second letter contained the news of his discovery of Malee and Lindy. As much as Kinley wanted to avoid looking at the pictures that were enclosed, she was drawn to them, by the end of the letter. It was so full of excitement and love for the little girl, who had celebrated her second birthday while Mario was there in Myanmar.

Three snapshots lay facedown in the envelope. The first one Kinley turned over was a headshot of Mario and Lindy. The same smile graced their faces. It was Tony's smile. Tears trailed down Kinley's cheeks, blurring her vision. *Who could not love that little child? Lindy is part of Mario.*

Feeling ashamed, she blubbered, too distraught to read the last letter. She needed to get busy, needed time to digest her emotions. With something so pressing on her mind, she knew she could zip through her housework in no time.

When her tasks were completed in record time and supper was baking in the oven, Kinley moved to the shade of the porch again with the remaining letter and a determination to keep an open heart and mind. As she ripped the flap from the envelope, several more photos fell out. Mario had written captions on the backs of them. On two pictures of him and Lindy, he had applied cartoon sticker bubbles that read, "Love at first sight" and "My surprise family, 1995."

A single sheet of paper on feminine-looking stationery was folded neatly inside. It was not in Mario's handwriting. Kinley quickly glanced at the signature before reading. It was from Malee.

> To Mr. and Mrs. Swenson, the guardians of my husband's son, Mario,
>
> I want to thank you for caring for Mario all these years after his mother's passing. He is a delightful, well-mannered boy. What a wonderful job you have done with him. Lindy and I fell in love with him from the moment we met. I also saw many of Tony's personality traits in him.
>
> Tony had plans for us to visit the States after the job in the Gulf of Mexico was complete, but alas, the God of all creation had other plans for him.
>
> Mario has extended an invitation for us to visit the farm one day, but we would not come without a proper welcome from your side of the family.
>
> With love for you and the awesome boy now part of our life, too,
>
> Malee

Kinley instantly had a yen to know this woman and her child better. She studied the enclosed pictures. Malee was beautiful, part oriental and possibly half American. *Starting now, I must make* amends with Mario. I will start with an invitation for Malee and the child to visit Swenson Farms.

Kinley was still sitting on the porch when the bus dropped Mario off. He waved goodbye to Lupita and started up the driveway, pulling an apple off a tree by the garden as he passed.

"How's my young world traveler?" she said, sauntering down the steps and greeting him with a warm hug. She sensed a little fear in him as she pulled him close. Rightfully so after the way she had been treating him and the others for the past week.

"Your letters came today. What nice pictures you sent. It looks like a beautiful country."

"I still have more pictures in my camera, but I …" He didn't finish.

She assumed he couldn't come up with the proper words without being rude or accusatory of her behavior. "Where's Hans and Bobby?"

"They both had activities going on. I'm supposed to tell you or Grandpa they need a ride home."

"Well, maybe we can get those pictures developed when we go to pick them up. I'll even pay extra and wait for them to be developed. Okay?" She smiled.

"Sure." He gave her a curious look.

"Mario, I've had lots of time to think this past week, and your letters today have made me realize how thankful I am to have three great teenage boys. You're all healthy, doing well in school, and finding your place in the world. What more could any mom or grandma want?"

"I've been very selfish and even a little jealous of your other family across the sea. Malee's letter indicates how much she values you and shows that she wants to grow her and Lindy's relationship with you.

"I could tell by her writing that she is a wonderful woman. I am ashamed to have judged her as I did. Can you forgive me, my sweet boy?" Her sincerity was reflected in the tears filling her eyes once again.

There was no hesitation from Mario. He rushed into her arms and clung to her, her face resting on his thick dark hair for the longest moment.

When the embrace was over, Kinley said, "Grab your camera and let's go get those pictures developed. I want to see and hear more about this little sister and her mom."

Mario hesitated, then asked, "While we're in Ames, can we see about getting me some new glasses? Mine are broken again. And I've glued them in several places already."

She replied, "How about if we try contact lenses this time? I believe you're more than ready for a change. I will further try to make amends for my behavior by sending Malee and Lindy an invitation to spend Christmas at Swenson Farms."

"You're the greatest, Grandma. I love you."

CHAPTER 33

The first significant snowfall came the first week of December, burying the last blooms of summer beneath massive piles of snowflakes. Dark burgundy mums stretched their shaggy heads above the twinkling white surface along one stretch of the driveway by the farmhouse. They were the only thing of color to have survived, but soon they too would succumb to the cold weight that covered them.

"Mario," his grandmother called as he rode by the house to take Windy for a short trot, "since Hans and Nels are busy in the barn, would you be a dear and ride these over to the Moraleses?" She handed him a canvas bag.

"What's in it?"

"Pumpkin bread for the holidays. I can probably fill the freezer with pumpkin goodies this year."

"I was headed that way anyhow." He hung the bag over the saddle horn and spurred Windy to action.

"Be careful, dear."

As an afterthought, he stopped, got out of the saddle, and broke off a large stem of the mums. Adding the flowers to the canvas bag, he remounted Windy.

The Moraleses' home was joyfully decorated outside with vigil lights and candy canes partway up the drive leading to the house. A string of red and green chili pepper lights stretched along the porch rail, and a green knit wreath with a velvet bow hung on the door.

Lupita answered his knock. "Come in, Mario. Aren't the decorations pretty?"

Inside, the tree, which was sitting in the front window, was wrapped with chili pepper lights, red and green baubles, angels, stars, doves, and lots of tinsel. Five stockings hung limp on the mantel, waiting for Santa to plump them up.

"Oh yes. Very pretty. This is from my mom," he said, extracting the flowers and handing Mrs. Morales the bag.

Mrs. Morales excitedly sniffed the contents inside. "Ah! Still warm from the oven. How nice. I believe there is enough to have a slice now. Will you join us?" she said, heading for the kitchen.

"No, thank you, Mrs. Morales. We have lots more at home."

He handed Lupita the wet bouquet. "And, these are what's left of the summer flowers, just for you."

She whispered, "Thank you," and startled him with her next move. She stood on tiptoes and planted a sweet kiss on his lips. It was the moment he had thought about and dreamt about, and it caught him off guard when it happened.

"Did I embarrass you, Mario?" she whispered, looking upward.

"Uh … no, of course not." His eyes followed her gaze. A small bundle of mistletoe hung from the overhead ceiling fan. He was about to return her kiss with one of his own but heard an "ahem" come from the corner by the stove. He had failed to notice that Lupita's grandmother was in the room. "Now I'm embarrassed," he whispered softly.

Lupita quickly retreated to where her abuela was sitting, swiftly applying a pair of needles attached to a string of yarn. Lupita grabbed a knit hat from the stack of garments next to her abuela and pulled it over her dark hair. "Look what my abuela has made," she said. "She is making Christmas gifts for everyone. Aren't they lovely?"

"Uh, yes," he said, not totally out of the clouds from the kiss. As he studied Lupita's beautiful face and the black tresses poking out from the soft pink hat, he was reminded of Lindy. "Could I buy one of those in the same color for my little sister, Lindy? Smaller, of course."

The old woman smiled. "How old is she?"

"Two and a half."

"I think there is enough yarn left for one that size," she said, not taking her eyes off her work.

"That's great. How much will it cost?"

The old woman dismissed the question with a wave of her hand. "Not much. I'll let you know."

Lupita whispered in her abuela's ear. When the old woman nodded in the affirmative, Lupita pulled a black knit garment from the pile, walked over to Mario, and sweetly wrapped the scarf around his neck. "Our present to you, dear friend."

"Thank you, Lupita and Grandma. I love it."

As he rode home, he adjusted the scarf to cover his face. *The scarf is nice, but I liked the kiss even better.*

His head still in the clouds, Mario didn't see Hans and Buck coming toward him until he was almost upon them. Buck was pulling the big sleigh his grandpa had built years ago. "Where are you going?" he said, reining Windy to a stop.

"I thought I'd take Little Henry for a ride. He's never been around snow before. This should be a real treat."

"Is that what you and Grandpa were doing in the barn when I left?"

"Yeah. It was pretty dusty, so I had to clean it up a little. Dad said Buck should be able to handle the load as long as there are only a few passengers. Do you remember when old Harriet and Bessie used to pull us around the farm?"

"I sure do."

"Yeah. Poor Harriet. She was stomping and carrying on when I left. I think she thought she was going to pull the sleigh. Grandpa says she's not good for much anymore but sleeping and eating."

"Hans, you're so transparent. Since when are you into entertaining little kids? You're not fooling me, pal. It's Lupita you want to snuggle with in the cold, right?" He saw Hans's cold rosy cheeks turn an even deeper red.

"So what if Lupita wants to come along?"

Mario realized it was out of jealousy he had made the remarks to Hans. Why should he be worried about Hans, when Lupita had just kissed him on the lips under the mistletoe? He changed the subject. "What's Bobby doing?"

"He and Dad went into town to settle up with Bobby's aunt and uncle from South Dakota. Dad didn't want them coming to the farm, so they decided to meet at the lawyer's office."

"Oh yeah? Well, you and Little Henry enjoy dashing through the snow. See you later." With a click of his tongue and a slight kick to Windy's sides, Mario headed home.

The mailman stopped and shouted out the window, "I left another letter from Burma in your box. Probably a Christmas card."

"Thank you, sir. Merry Christmas if I don't see you again."

Later in the afternoon, Mario joined Hans and Grandpa in the living room by a roaring fire in the stone fireplace.

"Why are you still wearing that neck scarf?" Hans chided.

"I'm cold. There's a chill in the air."

"Are you sure you're not coming down with something?" Mario's grandpa asked.

"Nah. I'll be fine." *I'm not coming down with something. I've already got it—a bad case of affection.*

"Did Little Henry have fun?" The question to Hans was only preliminary to what Mario really wanted to know.

"Yeah, he did. I let him hold onto the reins and think he was driving."

Mario waited for Hans to say more, but that was it. Finally, he just came right out and asked, "Did Lupita go?"

Hans answered with irritation in his voice, "Yes, and so did her abuela, if you must know. Lupita thought her abuela would enjoy it.

They sat in the back all bundled up, and the old lady shrieked and squealed with delight all the way."

Mario laughed loudly, envisioning the unromantic scene.

His grandfather even chuckled. "Was Buck able to handle the sleigh with that many people?"

"Yes, he did fine. Altogether, Lupita, the grandmother, and Little Henry probably don't weigh as much as me."

"What you did was really nice, Hans," Mario said with a smirk.

His grandmother walked in with a plate of Christmas cookies and joined them.

"How about your day, Nels? Did you get things settled with Bobby's relatives?" Grandma asked.

Grandpa seemed to tense up. "You mean those greedy vultures? They had a list of expenses as long as my arm: pain and suffering, gas money to drive down here, food they consumed, doctor's bills, funeral home charges, and so on. The lawyer was pretty sharp though; he only gave them money for any receipts they could produce, which they had for the cremation and autopsy bills only. I was very proud of Bobby. He asked if the lawyer would send a generous check to the homeless shelter and soup kitchen there in Ames. So proud of the boy," he repeated. "By the way, where is he? I know I brought him home."

Kinley said, "Carmen called and said Bobby may be late. He is helping Lupita search for Sunshine. The little jumper apparently got out again."

"When I brought the sleigh home," Hans said, "Bobby was just leaving for Senor's place. He had Ebony decorated with a red and green wreath and bells around his neck." Addressing his father, he said, "You must have gotten his hair cut while you were in town. I like the mullet on him. With that black leather jacket and boots, he was one cool-looking dude."

Mario was silent. *Now I have to keep my eye on Bobby too?*

Bobby jingled and pranced Ebony in front of the Moraleses'

farmhouse until Lupita looked out the window. He motioned for her to come outside.

She ventured out in a pink knit hat and a puffy coat in the same color. She clapped and danced with joy as Bobby strutted Ebony around the front yard.

"He is so beautiful. Can I ride him?"

"Sure," Bobby said. "Merry Christmas, Lupita." He slid off and helped her up.

"You did this just for me?" She smiled.

"Just for you!" he shouted, watching her ride down the driveway and back.

She stopped next to Bobby on the return and stroked Ebony's neck and sides. "Oh, he is magnificent."

Senor came from the barn with a rope in his hand. "Sunshine is missing. She must have jumped the fence again. She usually doesn't go far, but I could use some help finding her," he said.

Bobby pulled himself up behind Lupita. "We'll find her, Senor Henry." He reached down as Senor handed him the rope. Bobby made a *click, click* sound with his tongue and pulled on the right rein. Ebony obediently turned around, and they trotted off toward the fields.

"Sunshine likes those weeds in the ditch close to Tommy's place," Lupita said. "I've found her there several times."

"I used to like those weeds, too, until my dad caught me trying to smoke them one day." He laughed.

"Bobby!" The shocked look on her face as she turned around amused him.

He was laughing when he said, "I'm just joking. But it is some kind of wild hemp."

"Bobby, that's not funny." She jabbed an elbow in his midsection.

"I bet Sunshine is addicted," he continued to tease. She elbowed him again. "Yep, there she is," Bobby said, spotting the goat's white furry head poking through the thick stand of weeds.

"She'll run. Help me down. I can catch her," Lupita said.

"I wouldn't want you to ruin that pretty coat or hat." Before he dropped down from Ebony, on impulse, he awkwardly turned Lupita's face toward him and kissed her. He waited, expecting another elbow to his gut or a slap. But instead, her dark eyes drank in his face. He kissed her again, more tenderly this time, his arms sliding around her waist, pulling her close.

Sunshine had broken free of the dried vegetation in the ditch and was now headed for the open field, bleating, running, and leaping like a deer.

The sigh that came from deep within Bobby said it all; it was a passionate moment deflated by a frisky goat. "Why don't you slide off, Lupita, so Ebony can run faster? I'll catch her."

The goat was no match for the regal horse, who swiftly ran neck and neck with Sunshine, then cut in front of her, rearing his front feet, stopping her in her tracks, and holding her at bay by not giving her room to run in any direction. Bobby jumped down and slipped the rope around her neck.

Lupita came running across the field. She was out of breath by the time she reached them. "I … think … she was going home. She … does that sometimes. She … even puts herself … back in the barn." She gasped and panted.

Bobby swatted Sunshine on the rear when she bleated and looked up innocently at Lupita. He could swear the animal was mocking him. *Stupid goat.*

Bobby and Lupita walked the rest of the way to the house hand in hand and in silence, Bobby leading Ebony and Lupita dragging Sunshine by the rope.

The scene around the fireplace at the Swenson farm seemed the perfect ending to a hectic day, Mario thought as he took it in.

Bobby was stretched out in a recliner with his eyes closed.

Mario's grandmother was writing notes as she thumbed through a Christmas catalog. "Cherise, Malee, and Lindy are coming for Christmas," she said. "I think it's time to put up the tree."

"I was about to say the same thing," said Grandpa. "We'll take the sleigh and look for one after church tomorrow."

Hans snatched the last decorated cookie and devoured it.

"It sure doesn't take much to make you happy," Mario said to him. "Shouldn't you start watching your weight? Wrestling practice starts right after Christmas, you know."

"Not your concern," Hans mumbled with his mouth full.

"Come on, let's go to the barn and bring in the tree decorations. You coming, Bobby?"

"Nah. I'm pretty tired from chasing that goat all over creation. It feels very good here by the fire. I'll do my share of putting the tree together tomorrow," he said, closing his eyes again.

The little green-eyed monster of jealousy has surfaced again. I wonder what that sappy smile on his face is all about. If it's about Lupita, then his paradise here at Swenson Farms is about to be rocked.

Mario stood by the 1994 Mustang waiting for Hans and Bobby. Grandpa Fontanini had sent the car as a Christmas present for the three boys.

Aunt Cherise, Malee, and Lindy had driven the car all the way from Boston to deliver it instead of having it shipped. Grandpa and Emma had headed for a warmer climate to spend Christmas.

What a grand time Christmas had been. Malee and Lindy seemed to fit right in with their growing family. The little ones, Lindy, Enrique, and Tommy's five-year-old, Ross, kept the excitement alive. They built snowmen, rode around the farm in the sleigh, and hung their stockings on the fireplace mantel. Santa even made an appearance on Christmas Eve, much to their delight.

It was a sad time when the farmhouse emptied after everyone had rung in the New Year of 1996.

School was back in session. Mario had dibs on being the first to drive their new car to school.

As Mario waited for Hans and Bobby, the yellow school bus drove by the house without stopping because they weren't standing at the end of the driveway or running to catch it.

Our bus riding days are coming to an end. We are growing up, no longer little kids obeying bus rules, but teenagers trying to fit into the numerous stricter rules of community life.

I've experienced many changes in the last three years, some of them very painful, including the loss of my father and learning to live peacefully with my once archenemy, Bobby. But I feel that I am a stronger and wiser person now.

Senor's family coming to live permanently at the farm, and finding a little sister, Lindy, on the other side of the world, were definitely blessings for me in this complicated world.

I can't imagine the changes ahead as Swenson Farms evolves into the next generation.